"This is a terrible situation."

"The worst," Kim agreed. "And I want you to know I'd like it to continue. There's nothing I want to do that wouldn't seem empty if you weren't with me to share it." Kim waited, watching his eyes.

Slowly, a smile teased his mouth. "You're quite sure?"

"Quite."

Mark's smile faded, and he folded her closer, kissing her with a thoroughness that left her reeling. Then he raised his head. "These last few weeks have been pure misery.... Will you marry me, Kim?"

When, she wondered, had a street kid named Kim Wade turned so lucky? Her eyes welled up, and for once she didn't even try to stem the flow. "Of course I will!"

Dear Reader,

Like Kim's, my own wedding very nearly approached perfection. I wore a gown of summery organza and Venice lace that had been featured on the cover of *Bride's Magazine*. My six attendants were visions in pale yellow voile and large straw hats. The men were elegantly tuxedoed, the church was appropriately solemn, the day was brilliantly sunny.

But, oh, the reception! What a party that was! With two hundred guests, it included everything from the obligatory flank of aunts doing a line dance to a cigar-smoking family friend donning one of the bridesmaid's broad-brimmed hats and talking the bandleader into playing a striptease.

It was such a good time, in fact, that after bidding our guests farewell, my husband and I decided not to set out for Cape Cod immediately, as planned, but to hurry to my parents' house where we knew the party was about to shift. We arrived before anyone else, which naturally became the joke of the evening.

Unfortunately we stayed late, very late. We'd already arranged to take the ferry to Nantucket the next morning, and we'd reserved our room on the island for the week. But what we hadn't done was book our lodging for that night.

No problem, we'd thought. Cape Cod has thousands of motel rooms, right? What we were about to learn was that, late on a July night, every one of those rooms is occupied. And so we drove, drove the entire length of the Cape, drove nearly the entire night—before finally giving up and heading inland. What was worse, we couldn't even go to our own apartment since we'd let out-of-town guests stay there.

Funny, how we love to tell stories about the things that go wrong with seemingly perfect events. I suspect it's because we draw satisfaction from knowing we survived. And we did. After twenty-four years my husband and I are able to look back on our wedding-night wanderings with humor, secure in the knowledge that when romance and adversity tangle, deeper love is often the result.

Sincerely,

Shannon Waverly

TEMPORARY ARRANGEMENT
Shannon Waverly

Harlequin Books

TORONTO • NEW YORK • LONDON
AMSTERDAM • PARIS • SYDNEY • HAMBURG
STOCKHOLM • ATHENS • TOKYO • MILAN
MADRID • WARSAW • BUDAPEST • AUCKLAND

To Jim,
whose love and support make all things possible

ISBN 0-373-03259-5

Harlequin Romance first edition April 1993

TEMPORARY ARRANGEMENT

CHAPTER ONE

"MARK?"

"Who's this?"

"Hi. It's your sister."

"Miriam?"

"Surprise!"

Mark Johnson tossed aside the contract he was working on, removed his reading glasses and settled back with a stunned smile. "Good Lord! How the hell are you, Sis?"

"Oh, could be better, but let's never mind about me. How're you?"

"Fine. Busier than ever."

"Good, good. And how's that new job of yours going?"

"New job? Oh, with Brightman, Collins and Fuller?" Mark's smile drooped at the edges. He'd been with the law firm for two years. "Pretty well. I . . ." He paused, wondering if he should mention he was up for partnership. He wasn't supposed to know about it himself. "It's going very well."

"That's marvelous, Mark. Who would've thought it, huh, the way you and I were brought up? I'm proud of you. You know that, don't you?"

Mark glanced at a fuzzy snapshot sitting on his desk in a heavy sterling frame. It was the most recent picture he had of Miriam, taken at his college graduation nine years ago. She'd been thirty, blond and ripe then—and recently divorced from her second husband. Mark had been twenty-three and hungry, with law school on his mind and dreams of making it big burning in his gut. She was wearing a red dress with a low-cut flounced neckline. He had on a borrowed suit whose pants were too short. Their arms were around each other and they were smiling. She'd traveled up from Tucson for the occasion, a gesture he'd never forget. From there she'd moved on to New York—and he hadn't seen her since.

"So, what's up with you? And what is this could-be-better stuff?"

"Oh, nothing. I hate calling with my troubles, you know I do."

"Miriam, knock it off." Mark wasn't sure what he meant by that. Knock off the implication that she couldn't call him with her troubles? Or, knock off the pretense that she called him at all. They talked once, maybe twice, a year, if they were lucky.

But then, he didn't make much of an effort, either. Not that he didn't want to, but over the years they'd developed an understanding of sorts. They each had their lives and let the other be. But, Lord, she had to know he'd always be there for her.

"All right," she sighed. "All right." Another silence. Then, "My husband died, Mark."

Mark sat up like a shot. "Oh, Miriam! I'm so sorry." He thrust a hand through his hair. Of all times, why now? "Listen, babe. Don't you worry about a thing. I can be packed and on a plane in two hours." He grimaced as he thought of all the projects he'd have to put on a back burner. "You're not going to go through this alone."

Miriam coughed quietly. "Um . . . no. No, don't. That's not necessary. You see, um, Cliff died . . . not recently."

"What? What do you mean, not recently?"

"Well, he died . . . five months ago. But that's not why I'm calling," she added in a rush.

Mark clutched the back of his neck, his body going still as her message sank in. "Miriam, you didn't even think to call me about your husband's death?"

"I know, I know. But I hate bothering you. You're busy, and I didn't want you making an expensive trip just for a funeral."

"For heaven's sake, Miriam, I'm your brother!" He waited for a response, trying to deny the anger and hurt he was feeling. And the sense of loss. He'd never met Cliff and had been hoping Miriam might have brought him out for a visit this summer, now that he had this big house.

"Well, I'm sorry," Miriam said. "I guess I wasn't thinking too straight at the time, the shock and all."

Mark conceded the point with a doubtful sigh. "So, what did he die of? Cliff couldn't have been that old."

"It was a car accident. He died instantly—no suffering, thank heaven. Anyway, what I started to say was, life's been kind of lonely around here since then, and to make a long story short... Mark, would you be very upset having your big sister as a neighbor?"

Mark felt his eyes bugging out and didn't even want to guess at his heart rate. "Here? In Colorado Springs?"

"Uh-huh. Oh, I know I left home when you were only ten, and I haven't been the greatest at keeping in touch. But we're still brother and sister, Mark, and like it or not, we're the only family we've got, and frankly I miss the hell out of you, and I'm hoping it's not too late for us to be close. I guess Cliff's death got me thinking about how short life is and...and about what's really important, if you know what I mean."

Mark pinched the bridge of his nose. Yes, he knew.

"So, I was wondering if you'd mind me moving out there."

"Are you kidding? I'd love it."

"Really?"

Mark was about to reply with another ready affirmative when he hesitated. Did he really want his sister back in his life? He and Miriam had parted years ago. They'd led separate and very different lives, and he wasn't sure she'd fit into his anymore. He was entering the proverbial fast lane—or as fast as it got in a city of almost 300,000. Miriam, though she'd always been a survivor, hadn't come nearly as far. She'd never finished high school, never pursued a career, and all her husbands had been blue-collar workers. She'd probably feel awkward among his friends, and he was afraid he wouldn't have time to help her adjust.

On the other hand, how could he refuse? She was his sister. No matter how many miles or years had come between them, she was still his first allegiance.

"Mark, are you still there?"

"Uh, yes. Of course I'd love to have you living here. It'll be wonderful. I've always wanted you closer."

"You can't imagine how happy that makes me." Miriam quietly blew her nose. "Now, I don't want this to be any bother for you. I'm selling the house here in Brooklyn, so I'll have plenty of money to set myself up in a nice apartment when I get there, but I do have one favor to ask."

Inexplicably Mark tensed, waiting for a hitch.

His reaction surprised and dismayed him. Miriam wasn't like that. Not with him, at least. He knew she wasn't an angel. Their early lives had been difficult, and they'd had to make their way however they could. In Miriam's case, that had sometimes meant using people. But she'd never used him and never would. That was at the foundation of their mutual understanding, at the heart of their loyalty and love.

"Would you send me some local newspapers?" she asked. "I want to check the real estate and job ads to get an idea of what's available out there."

Mark's shoulders sagged with relief—and guilt for having doubted her. "They'll be in the mail tomorrow, but please don't feel you have to rush. I have plenty of room here. You can stay with me.''

"Oh, I couldn't.''

"Of course you can, and you will. I insist you stay here while you're...looking...'' Mark's words slowed as if they were becoming mired in some black sticky substance. "Miriam, didn't Cliff have a daughter when you married him?''

"Um, yes.'' The line hummed with taut silence.

"Has she gone to live with a relative? An aunt or something?''

"No, poor kid. Kim hasn't got any relatives.''

Mark picked up a pen and fiddled with its cap. "Then . . . will she be coming with you?''

"Afraid so. That's why I hate to impose. If it was just me . . .''

Though he didn't much care for the way Miriam had gotten herself invited and *then* told him about the girl, he couldn't very well object. They came as a package. "Miriam, don't be silly. I have four bedrooms.''

"It'll only be a short stay. A few days, till we get a place of our own.''

"Take all the time you need.''

"Thanks, love.''

"Don't mention it. So, when can I expect you?''

"Let's see. Today's Wednesday . . . I sign over the deed a week from today. . . . How about the Friday after?''

"That soon?'' Mark gulped. Somehow, he'd been thinking in terms of a month or two, when all this promotion business would be over. Right now he was working sixty-, sometimes seventy-hour weeks. How was he supposed to fix up two spare bedrooms when he was keeping that kind of schedule? How would he squeeze two more people into his life when he was embroiled in the most complicated case of his career? And then there was Suzanne, who took up what little time he had left. As if that weren't enough, a week after Miriam's proposed arrival, he was hosting a party here, a party he wasn't ready for. No, they'd just have to decide on a later date.

"A week and two days from now?" he murmured doubtfully.

"Thanks, Mark," Miriam said quickly. "I'm in your debt forever"

Mark started to protest, but she'd already hung up.

THE FOLLOWING WEDNESDAY, the ten employees of Wheeler Auto Sales in Brooklyn threw Kim Wade a going-away party during lunch hour. There was a raspberry cheesecake, champagne, and lots of hugs and kisses.

Kim stood by her desk, accepting their good wishes and feeling increasingly uneasy. This move didn't make sense. Her life was here. Her friends, her job, her neighborhood.

"I had no idea you were thinking of moving," one of the salesmen complained. "When did this come about?"

"Only a couple of weeks ago, Tom."

"Geez, Kim. Colorado? Why so far?"

"My stepmother was born in Colorado and still has family there."

"So?"

"So, now that my father's gone, there isn't much left for her here, and she wants to go back. She asked me to go with her."

"And just like that, you're going?"

It wasn't just like that. There had been questions and arguments and long doubt-filled nights, but Kim replied with an eloquent snap of her fingers.

The salesman shook his head, still disbelieving. "When are you leaving?"

"Friday."

"*This* Friday?"

"Uh-huh. We're all packed and ready to go."

"But...do you know if you'll be able to get work? Do you have a place to stay?"

"Hey, Tom," a smoke-husky voice called across the office. "There's a customer out on the lot eyeballing the red Mazda." Charlotte was Wheeler Auto's bookkeeper and one of Kim's oldest friends. It was Charlotte who'd recommended her for this job when the previous secretary retired ten months ago. At the time Kim had been working as a waitress, a job only slightly better than the factory position that had preceded it.

The salesman sighed resignedly. "Well, take care, Kim. We're gonna miss you."

He was the last person to leave the office. Everyone else had returned to their various jobs. When he was gone, Charlotte cleared a spot on her desk and sat down, her black miniskirt riding high on her thigh.

"Thanks for the rescue," Kim said.

"No problem. I figured you were sick of answering questions." She lit a cigarette and blew out a thin stream of smoke. "But I have to admit, I've got a few myself."

Kim tossed her plastic cup into a wastebasket. "Like?"

"Like, what's in it for you?"

"In moving? Gee, I don't know. Why would I want to leave Brooklyn and go out West where the air is clean, there's far less crime, more opportunity, and I have family?"

Charlotte squinted at her through a haze of smoke. "Family? Are we talking about the same old bat who slapped you silly that day you lost your paycheck?"

A knot pulled tight in Kim's stomach. "That was six years ago, Charlotte."

"So? I still think she had a nerve hitting you. She'd only just married your father, remember?"

Yes, Kim remembered. She'd been sixteen back then, sixteen and breathlessly eager for the mother she'd never had, for the shopping trips, the conversations about makeup and boys and physical changes that couldn't be discussed with a father. So eager...

What she'd got instead was neglect. There had been no place for her in that new marriage. She was too old to be cute, too young to be turned out. The only attention she did remember getting was on payday.

But Kim refused to encourage her friend. Charlotte didn't need much to set her off on one of her evil-stepmother harangues.

"That was an isolated incident," Kim lied, sitting on the desk, too. "Miriam hasn't hit me since."

"She hasn't exactly been Mother Teresa, either, and if you ask me, her buddy-buddy behavior these last few weeks is awfully screwy, especially when you consider how vile she got right after your father died."

Kim ducked her head, her long auburn hair falling forward. She was trying to forget that time. But Charlotte was right; even before Kim had come to terms with her grief, Miriam had started urging her to leave. Wasn't it time she got out on her own? Miriam had contended. Wouldn't she like to be married? *She* had been married at Kim's age.

At first Kim thought Miriam was kidding. Married? Good heavens, she wasn't even dating anyone. But when she refused to leave, Miriam's urgings turned abusive. They argued continually until finally Miriam began threatening to lock her out.

Kim was stunned. She'd considered moving out in the past but had always been asked to stay. She didn't understand why Miriam was suddenly so eager now. And where would she go? How would she support herself without training and a better job? Furthermore, why *should* she go? Wasn't this her house, too?

Miriam's reply still had the power to upset her.

As if reading her thoughts, Charlotte said, "Miriam's signing over the house to the new owner today, huh?"

Kim nodded. "She's at the bank now."

"I still can't believe it."

Kim dug down for the toughness she'd learned to hide behind years ago, whenever the pain cut too close. "It wasn't much of a house," she replied, lifting her chin. "Just a crumbling duplex in the middle of Brooklyn."

"But you grew up there. It belonged to your grandmother. She left it to your father with the hope he'd pass it on to you."

"And sometime during their marriage my father decided to add Miriam's name to the deed."

"Probably one night when she got him pie-eyed."

"Charlotte, please."

"Sorry. But he did drink, and she encouraged it. And I still think it's screwy, Miriam inheriting everything—the house, his insurance, his pension. There's got to be a loophole somewhere."

Kim chewed on her lower lip, wondering if she should admit that she'd had similar thoughts. "No, Charlotte. No loopholes. I contacted a lawyer about a month ago to check it out."

Charlotte turned sharply. "You did?"

"Mmm. Well, not a real lawyer, just one of those free advocacy groups you see advertised on the subway. But they were very nice, and they came to the conclusion that everything was aboveboard and airtight. I don't have a ghost of a case against Miriam."

Charlotte swore under her breath.

"Don't, Charlotte. It wasn't her fault. It was my father who put things in her name. Besides, she's offered to share the money once we get to Colorado."

Charlotte snorted. "I'll believe that when I see it."

"She will. She said I'll finally be able to go to school, and she'll pay."

"Whoop-de-do." Charlotte made a sardonic circle in the air with her index finger. "She was the reason you never went in the first place. All that room-and-board she was charging you, there was no way you could save for tuition."

"They *needed* the money," Kim replied defensively. "My father was laid off half the time, and Miriam couldn't work because of her heart. Besides, I didn't mind. I felt useful, a necessary part of the family."

Charlotte turned and pinned Kim with a sharp look. "You have an excuse for everything, don't you?"

Kim's chest rose and fell with quick anxious breaths. "Yes."

"Why?"

"Why?" Kim swallowed. "Because... because, Charlotte, life would simply be unbearable if I didn't. Now, if you'll excuse me, it's time I cleaned out my desk."

THE PHONE RANG late Friday afternoon, just as Mark came dashing in from work.

"Hello."

"Hi, how're you doing, love?"

"Miriam?" He dropped his briefcase and frowned at his watch. "Shouldn't you be on a plane?"

"That's why I'm calling. There's been a slight change of plans. You know that buyer I had for my house? Well, the jerk backed out of the deal at the last minute."

"Oh. Oh, I'm sorry. Tough break, Sis."

"Yeah, well... story of my life. But that's okay. Another couple came by this afternoon, and they seemed pretty interested. Already put down a binder."

Mark's eyebrows shot up. "That's amazing. I thought the housing market was in a slump."

"Mmm. The only trouble now is, I'll have to stick around here a few more weeks."

Mark breathed a sigh of relief. This was just the break he needed. "No problem, Miriam. My door's open whenever you're ready."

"Glad to hear that, because Kim's flown on without me. She'll be landing around seven-thirty, your time."

Mark fell into the chair by the phone. "Kim'll be here tonight? Alone?"

"Mmm. I figured you wouldn't mind, since you were expecting us, anyway."

"She's on her way—alone?"

"Well, she was all packed and ready to go, and I saw no reason for her to wait for me. Besides, we had economy tickets that couldn't be exchanged. Bad enough mine's gone to waste..." She paused. "You don't mind, do you?"

Now she asks? Now? When the girl's already in the air?

"Uh-oh. You do mind."

Mark dragged a hand down his tired face. This wasn't the arrangement he'd expected. Taking in Kim along with Miriam was one thing; Miriam would be responsible for her. But Kim alone? He didn't have the time or the patience for this arrangement, and Miriam had no right foisting it on him.

"Mark, don't worry. Kim won't be any trouble, and I'll be there before you know it." Miriam coughed quietly. "But I do have one favor to ask before she gets there."

"Oh?" Mark bristled.

"Could you make sure she gets busy settling in as soon as possible?"

"I'm not sure I understand."

"Well, I'm hoping she'll get real involved in things—meeting people, learning her way around, even checking out apartments for us. I want her to feel she has a real stake in our new life, y'know?"

"I think so."

"But I especially want her to get settled into a nice job. A job's so important to a person's sense of belonging, don't you think?"

Mark's head was beginning to feel stuffed with fuzz. "Wait. Hold it. I'm a little confused. Shouldn't I be registering her for school or something?"

"School? Regular school?" Miriam suddenly cackled. "Mark, Kim doesn't go to school. She graduated already."

Mark thrust his fingers through his hair, his pulse quickening. "Really? Where'd the time go? When you married Cliff, she was just a kid." He'd expected to play uncle to a teenager, but a *young* teenager, one whose problems centered on school dances and acne. But Kim must be eighteen, maybe even nineteen. A girl her age had problems of a different sort. Drugs. Cars. Birth control.

"I should level with you, Mark. I suspect Kim isn't too thrilled about this move and may try to return to New York."

"Why would she do that?"

"It's all she knows. But this city's a dead end." Miriam exhaled a shuddering sigh. "Keep her there—could you do that for me, please? Get her involved right away so she won't even think about returning. There's nothing for her here, just dead-end friends and more dead-end jobs."

"Miriam, you sound as if the girl might try to skip town."

"Sorry. I'm probably overreacting, but it's only because I love her so much and want the best for her, and this move *is* for the best. In Colorado there's bound to be more opportunity for her to make something of herself. That's my dream, anyway."

The fuzz in Mark's head had bloomed to a full throbbing ache now. Miriam said she wanted Kim to become "involved" so she wouldn't run back to New York, but what she really meant was for *him* to become involved—in Kim's life. Well, he couldn't do it. And he wouldn't. If Miriam had aspirations for this kid, who apparently had no drive or direction of her own, well, she'd just have to get out here and work on them herself.

One thing he would do, though—he'd certainly encourage Kim to start learning her way around. She was old enough to take care of herself. Tough enough, too, he'd bet. Probably too tough. Coming from Brooklyn, she'd probably find the wholesome small-town atmosphere of Colorado Springs one big yawn. Well, he had his own life to tend to, his own aspirations, and the sooner the kid moved out of his house, the better off he'd be.

"I'll see what I can do," Mark replied determinedly.

"Thanks. I owe you a big one."

Mark was beginning to believe she was right.

KIM WISHED she had a cigarette. Of course, she hadn't smoked in years and wasn't about to resume the habit now, but the desire was there nonetheless, growing in direct proportion to her conviction that this trip was a mistake.

The plane bumped through a pocket of turbulence, and she gripped the armrests hard, peeking at the woman beside her. She'd never been on a plane before, and wasn't certain if what they were experiencing was normal. But the woman just kept on reading. She'd been reading the entire journey, a fact Kim regretted. It would've been nice to have someone to talk to.

But then, what would she have said? That she was flying out to Colorado to stay with an "uncle" she didn't even know? Surely the woman would've asked why, and then what would she have told her? Kim wasn't at all certain.

Oh, she'd heard Miriam's reasons, but what she didn't know was Miriam's secret agenda, and there usually was a secret agenda when Miriam was involved.

Kim closed her eyes and searched for a more charitable attitude. She didn't want to be distrustful. It was a terrible way to start a new life.

But growing up as she had, distrust was now second nature. And Charlotte was right. This about-face of Miriam's *was* a bit peculiar.

Kim let her head rest against the cool vibrating window. No, she wouldn't think so negatively. Miriam's enthusiasm had been too genuine these past few weeks as they'd packed their belongings, looked through real-estate ads and talked about the future. Surely everything would turn out as planned. Kim had to think positive. This move was exciting, an adventure, the beginning of the rest of her life.

Instead of excited, though, Kim only felt scared. Where in hell were they, anyway? South Dakota? Nebraska? Below, everything was sand-colored and empty and had been for hours. She felt lost, invisible, hurtling through the sky without a single tie to bring her down.

This trip was such an uncharacteristic leap of trust for her. As far back as she could remember, she'd depended on no one but herself. Who else was there? But now she was flying to the back of beyond and gambling her future on the word of a woman who, in the past, had only looked out for herself. Was she crazy?

Charlotte thought she was. But then, Charlotte had parents. Charlotte had aunts, uncles, cousins and a fiancé. She hadn't a clue how painful aloneness could be, or how easy it was to forgive a stepmother who claimed to be turning a new leaf.

Kim chewed on a knuckle as she stared down at the sand-colored nothingness, her mind traveling back to the evening when Miriam did her strange turnaround....

"This isn't right, us fighting. With your father gone, we're all the family we've got, Kim. It's time we pulled together."

Kim had waited too long to hear sentiments like those. She wasn't about to let common sense spoil them now, or the surprise and joy she'd felt when Miriam told her about a brother in Colorado. A stepuncle to Kim.

"I've always hoped to be closer to him, Kim, and I've been thinking, if I sold the house here, we could move—both of us. The move would be as much for your benefit as for mine. He's real smart and he has connections. He can help you with whatever plans you have, including that training you've always talked about. And I'd help, too, of course. I'd have the money from selling the house. But more important, we'd all be together. You, me, Mark. We'd be the start of a new family.''

Kim had been astounded. She'd begun dreaming about becoming a professional certified nanny when she was fifteen, but Miriam had never valued education, especially education you had to pay for. It didn't matter that the training lasted less than six months and wasn't all that expensive. Miriam's attitude had always been that, after high school—if you were lucky enough to finish high school— you simply went out to work, and that was that.

Besides, Miriam thought a nanny was a silly thing to want to be. Girls raised on the streets of Brooklyn didn't suddenly turn into Mary Poppins, she said. What would Kim do in a fancy house? How would she act among rich people? Wasn't she afraid she'd make a fool of herself?

The derision, the lack of confidence and support—that was what hurt most of all, Kim reflected, not the fact that after room and board was paid and necessities bought, she never had anything left to save for tuition. She wouldn't have cared if she'd had to work at the same dead-end job the rest of her life—if only she'd had someone at home pulling for her.

But now all that was changed. Miriam had gone from adversary to ally. She was offering Kim the promise of family and belonging. And that, *that* was why Kim had gotten on this plane back at Kennedy. She wanted to believe the promise was real.

Unfortunately Kim's optimism was riding atop a sea of uncertainties, the most disturbing of which was probably Theodore. Theodore was the man Miriam had started seeing six weeks after Kim's father had died. Miriam claimed they weren't serious, but Kim suspected otherwise. Too many nights she'd come home from work to find the table set for two—only to be told she wasn't one of the two. Together, Miriam and Theodore had a special knack for making her feel unwanted. Now Kim feared he'd follow them out to Colorado and Miriam's promises of a new shared life would go up in smoke. And where would that leave her?

I should've stayed in New York, she thought, exhausted from weeks of emotional vacillation. She didn't know a single person where she was headed. Back East, she had a few friends, a perfectly good training center and the upper East Side where she'd always dreamed of landing a post. Charlotte was right. Boarding this plane had been an act of insanity.

The pilot came on the intercom then, informing his passengers they'd be landing in fifteen minutes. The weather in Colorado Springs, he said, was clear, dry and sixty degrees.

Kim sat up. Fifteen minutes? She folded her arms over her waist where knots of tension were suddenly making her nauseated. She wasn't ready to meet the stranger who was supposed to be her uncle. She wasn't ready to live in a strange house, in a city she didn't know. Not alone.

She closed her eyes, praying that she and her uncle would get along. She'd never been close to her father—how could you be close to someone who wasn't even aware of you?— and frankly she wasn't sure she knew how to get on with an older man. To make matters worse, this older man was a lawyer. What would they ever talk about?

She lifted her handbag off the floor and pried out her compact from the clutter. After a week of sleepless nights, she looked pale and tired. Even her long auburn hair looked tired, hanging in lank lusterless spirals, the last reminders of a perm she preferred to forget.

Just then the plane banked. She shoved the compact into her bag and gripped the armrests. Still, she couldn't resist looking out the window. Below, the city of Colorado

Springs sprawled like a vast, low rug at the foot of the Rockies. Kim drew a breath, awestruck by the massive wall of snowcapped mountains that formed the city's backdrop.

When the plane banked again, she wondered if the travel-sickness pill she'd taken five hours earlier had worn off and that was why she was experiencing this terrible wooziness. Despite her physical discomfort, she kept her face pressed to the glass, her heart singing with excitement. This was the beginning of the rest of her life, and everything would work out just fine. She'd *make* it work.

They landed smoothly, and before long she was on her feet, retrieving her carryon from the compartment overhead. The close press of bodies, reaching, slipping on coats and jostling, made Kim dizzier still. Perhaps she should have eaten, she thought. She dropped into an aisle seat, fighting a wave of nausea.

No! This wasn't the time to cave in. *Think strong,* she reprimanded herself. *Think tough, nobody's fool...*

She rose determinedly and slipped on her coat, then flowed with the crowd down the long carpeted tube from the plane into the airport, trying to appear as if she knew exactly what she was doing. She'd watch the woman in front of her, she decided, to see how she got her luggage.

But it seemed luggage was not the first item on the agenda. With an aching heart, Kim watched the other passengers spill into the lobby and scatter to embrace family and friends.

Well, she did have a stepuncle somewhere in this crowd, she thought philosophically. She scanned the glass-walled area, wondering how she was supposed to recognize him. Miriam hadn't even had a picture.

Almost immediately her eyes locked on a man whose eyes were already locked on her. For a moment she could neither move nor breathe.

He looked away abruptly, across the dispersing crowd, as if dearly hoping to find someone else. But when he finished his search, Kim was still standing there, the only person still unclaimed. With a frown darkening his face, his strode toward her.

"Kimberly Wade?"

"Mr. Johnson?"

They eyed each other guardedly. He was at least six feet tall, had Miriam's deep azure eyes and hair the same light brown tipped with gold. Kim had expected him to resemble his sister somewhat, but what she hadn't expected was for him to be so young. Or so handsome.

Good Lord! she thought, fighting another bout of dizziness. Someone had poured a Mel Gibson lookalike into a Pierre Cardin suit and, probably laughing hysterically, dropped him right in the middle of her wretched life!

CHAPTER TWO

"HOW WAS YOUR FLIGHT?" he asked, running a quick but thorough survey of her appearance. He wasn't smiling.

Kim blinked through her surprise and felt heat wash into her cheeks. "Pardon me?"

"Your flight. How was it?"

"Oh. Good, except there was a snowstorm moving into the Northeast when we took off. That made me kind of nervous." Kim couldn't take her eyes off the man standing before her. This was her new uncle? This Adonis in a suit and tie?

"Well, I think you'll be pleasantly surprised by the weather here." His voice was a warm mellow rumble. "March in Colorado Springs is mild and dry. We're a front-range city. On the edge of the plains. I hope you weren't expecting Aspen."

"What?" With a start, Kim realized her mind had wandered again. She saw a frown veeing down over his nose. Knots of nervousness tightened in her stomach. He didn't like her. She could tell. It was usually his kind who didn't, too. His face had a certain bronzed glow that she'd learned in high school meant, "I've just been skiing—and you haven't." His features were too smoothly handsome, teeth even and white, his nose never broken. It was the sort of face you didn't often find where she'd grown up.

She flicked her head and lifted her chin reflexively. "I hope you haven't been waiting long."

"No." Again he gave her a quick, slightly incredulous sweep. "Your flight was right on time."

The heat in her cheeks deepened as she realized he was checking out her clothes. Her boss had told her to travel comfortably. Jeans and a sweater would do, and Kim had taken his advice. But at the last minute Miriam had convinced her to exchange her sneakers and parka in favor of her high-heeled boots and long black coat. To "dress up" the outfit.

When she'd bought the coat, the salesgirl had assured her no one would ever be able to tell it wasn't real leather. Mark Johnson could, Kim thought, increasingly self-conscious.

"Oh, here." He held out a small plush bear wearing a T-shirt with the word "Colorado" across the front. "A little something to welcome you."

Kim's heart warmed, until she realized how unenthusiastic he was. He might've been handing her a tissue to blow her nose, and before she could even say thank-you, he asked, "Do you have any other luggage?"

"Yes," she replied dejectedly.

He took her carryon from her. "Shall we get it then?" In spite of his small kindnesses, everything about him wanted to withdraw from her. His face was expressionless, his eyes evasive, and he walked as if he was trying to leave her in his dust. Her hopes of finding a caring relative in this man began to fall apart.

"Miriam tells me you're a lawyer," she said, trying to match his stride. She thought he nodded. "Do you have a specialty?"

"What?"

Kim swallowed. "Do you specialize?"

"Oh. I'm a contract lawyer."

She plodded on. "That must be interesting."

"Sometimes. Mostly it's tedious and time-consuming. In fact, Kimberly, I have to warn you, I won't be able to spend nearly as much time with you as I'd like. I've been working ungodly hours lately."

"Oh." She gave him a sidelong peek. He didn't look very disappointed. In fact he looked rather relieved, and it occurred to her that perhaps he was using work as an excuse.

"That's okay," she said over the lump forming in her throat. "I have things to do, anyway."

They reached the luggage conveyor. "Yes, I know. I wish I could help personally..." His tone of regret was pitifully shallow. "I've done the next best thing, though, and called a friend who manages rental properties. He'll take you around whenever you're ready. Tomorrow, if you'd like."

Tomorrow? She hadn't even got into his house yet, and already he was showing her the door.

"Miriam also told me you need to find a job, so I've called someone to help in that department, too. A career counselor. You can drop by his office on Monday."

Kim passed a shaky hand over her eyes. "Why a career counselor?"

"Oh, they help people explore careers, discover aptitudes..."

"I know what they do. I asked you why."

"Well, instead of going off half-cocked looking for a job, wouldn't you rather know what interests you first?"

"I already know..." She paused, frowning. This man didn't know a thing about her and apparently didn't want to. All he wanted was to shuffle her on her way.

She clamped her mouth shut and stared at the luggage gliding by. *I should've stayed in New York,* she told herself for the hundredth time that day, and unexpectedly she blurted, "Mr. Johnson, this really isn't necessary."

"What isn't?"

"The trouble I'm putting you to. I—I can stay at a motel. Or even better, why don't I take the next flight back?"

That made him turn. Swiftly. "I can't let you do that."

"Why not?"

She noticed his mouth twitch. "Well, that just wouldn't be hospitable, would it?"

"I appreciate your concern," she said dryly, "but really I should go." Kim had no idea how she'd pay for a return flight, but she knew she didn't want to stay here.

"Sorry, Kimberly, but you can't leave. I—I promised Miriam I'd take good care of you until she got here. She warned me that . . . that you might feel you were imposing, coming here without her, and you might offer to stay somewhere else. She made me promise I'd keep you from running off until she arrived." He tried to smile.

"I'm not running off, Mr. Johnson. I'm simply going back home for a while. I'll return with Miriam."

"Kimberly, enough!" He sounded as if he were talking to a child. Under his smooth bronzed facade, she could see he was angry, frustrated and tired, and suddenly the absurdity of her situation hit her like a physical blow.

"Why are you calling me Kimberly?" she railed. "It's Kim. Just plain Kim."

He thrust his fingers through his thick sandy hair in a gesture of exasperation. "Fine. Kim."

She glanced away, feeling lost, disoriented, and dizzy again.

"Look, I realize this isn't New York, but the city does have its charms. Can't you at least give it a try?"

Just then, her suitcase rode past. She lunged forward and swung it to the floor.

"This is all," she bit out, not answering his question.

"Fine." He picked up the heavy bag as if it were an empty sack and started for the exit. "My car's in the lot across the road. Follow me."

For a moment, Kim hesitated, thinking again of how much better she'd feel returning home. As if reading her mind, Mark wrapped his free arm around her waist and gave a small tug. "Right this way." The glass doors opened onto the cool March evening.

Out on the dusky sidewalk Kim stepped free of his hold and stood for a moment gazing at the mountain range in the distance, silhouetted against a deep indigo sky. She'd never been so far from home before, and though she was trembling with insecurity, she'd never beheld anything more beautiful.

She was embarrassed by a yawn. "What time is it, Mr. Johnson?"

"Seven-forty, but your body thinks it's nine-forty." He took her arm, obviously impatient to keep moving.

At first Kim resisted his urging, but she knew she couldn't do anything about returning to New York tonight. Surrendering peacefully was probably the best move. Then, after a good night's sleep, she'd reexamine her options.

"By the way, the name's Mark," he said crisply. "Do you feel comfortable with that?"

She nodded uncomfortably. She wished he'd let her call him Mr. Johnson or even Uncle Mark. She needed something to wedge between herself and this man who was far too attractive for her peace of mind.

He stopped at a dark blue BMW and unlocked the door. "You can get in," he said brusquely, then went around and put the bags in the trunk.

Kim slid into the soft leather seat and closed her eyes. She was feeling dizzy again, light-headed. Yes, this was best, going along quietly and getting a good night's sleep.

They drove in silence while the city scrolled by. Shopping districts. Quiet residential sections. She wanted to pay closer attention, but her eyes were too heavy.

"A pity Miriam couldn't come with you."

Kim blinked sleepily. "Yes."

"How is she these days?"

Kim heard a softness in his voice that hadn't been there before. "She's . . . fine."

"Really? I worry about her sometimes."

A wave of resentment rippled through Kim. Miriam was the last person anyone should worry about.

"How's her health?"

She looked out the side window. Although Miriam claimed to have a bad heart, Kim knew better. A year ago, out of concern, she'd called Miriam's doctor. "Fine," she replied.

"Good. And financially? Does she seem to be managing?"

Fortunately they were pulling into a driveway then and Kim was able to let the subject slide. She didn't like the negative feelings that had begun to rise inside her. "This your place?"

"Yes, ma'am."

It was a large traditional-looking house, white, two-storied, squarish and friendly. "Very nice," she murmured, following him up the lighted walk. "By the way, do you have a wife?"

"Not the last time I looked, though some women have accused me of being married to my work."

She mounted the front steps, wondering who these women were. Wondering, too, why he wasn't married. He looked to be in his early thirties and certainly was a head-turner. Prime marriage material, in her estimation.

Inside the foyer he set down her bags and flicked a switch that lit two lamps in the adjacent living room.

"You live here all by yourself? Holy..." Kim turned slowly, awed by the size and elegance of the place.

"Hmm. I bought it about a year ago. Usually I'm not impulsive about decisions this big, but I was driving by one day and it just sort of grabbed me." He said something about his job and wanting a place with style, but Kim was only half listening. She'd caught a glimpse of herself in a mirror and the sight made her start. How strained she looked from tension! How pinched and pale! No wonder Mark had been giving her such strange looks.

"Let's take your bags straight up to your room," she vaguely heard him say. "I imagine you'll be wanting to get some sleep, which is just as well, since . . ."

His words were becoming fainter, garbled, dreamlike. The next thing Kim knew, the floor was rushing up to meet her.

KIM OPENED HER EYES to find Mark's worried face about four inches from hers. At first, thinking she was dreaming, she smiled, then reality set in and she bolted upright. At least that was her intent.

"Lie still," he cautioned softly.

She realized she was lying on a sofa and he was sitting beside her. Her coat was tossed over a nearby chair, and her boots had been removed, exposing the hole in the toe of her right sock.

"Here, take a sip." He lifted her head and touched a glass to her lips. Kim coughed as the fiery liquid burned a path down her throat.

"What *is* that, nitroglycerin?"

"Sorry, I'm all out."

She took another sip, becoming aware of how close they were sitting. His face wasn't perfect, she noticed with relief. He had a small oval mole on his right cheek, just to the side of what might be a laugh line. She sipped again, liking the warmth spreading through her.

He'd removed his suit jacket and loosened his tie. He was solidly built, she noted, with shoulders broad enough to shelter a woman all the days of her life. And he smelled wonderful—like dependability itself.

Kim jiggled her head to shake some sense into it. Good Lord, her fainting spell had turned her brain to mush.

Mark eased her head back to the pillow. "When was the last time you ate?"

Kim shrugged, although she knew perfectly well that nervousness had kept her from eating all that day, and in fact, she hadn't eaten well for a week. As if to prove the point, her stomach chose that very moment to growl.

"You should've told me you were running on empty, Kim. We could've grabbed something at the airport." With cool soothing fingers, he combed her tangled hair away from her face.

Kim ran her tongue over her parched lips, feeling strangely uncomfortable. "I'm not hungry, just dizzy."

"It happens to some people, the quick ascents and descents in a plane. Do you always feel dizzy after flying?"

"I . . . I've never noticed it before." Her cheeks grew hot. Did she dare admit how inexperienced she was? "Actually, that...that was my first plane trip." The face she looked up into showed no signs of amusement or derision, as she'd expected.

"Were you nervous?"

"A little."

He nodded, seeming to understand. His eyes were incredibly blue seen this close, with a mesmerizing starburst of violet spikes around the iris, and his lips were firm and well-shaped.

"Of course, you just might be experiencing a Rocky Mountain high," he said, smiling. Yes, those *were* laugh lines, she realized.

"A what?"

"You're at an altitude much higher than you're used to. Even with a full stomach, you might still be hanging on to walls for the next few days."

"Wonderful."

"Don't worry. You'll adjust. Just take it easy, okay? No heavy exercise and stay off the nitroglycerin." He stood up and grinned. "Here." He flipped her the TV remote control. "I'm going into the kitchen to get us something to eat. Be here when I return." He walked away, the muscles of his tapering back shifting sinuously under his white shirt.

They spent a quiet hour, watching sitcoms and sipping chicken-noodle soup. When the hour was up, her stomach felt much better, and she was able to eat half a corned-beef sandwich. Before she finished it, however, her head was nodding.

"Okay, young lady. I'd say it's time you called it a day."

She didn't protest when he helped her to her feet and all the way up the stairs. She couldn't remember the last time she'd received such attention. With his arm still looped around her waist for support, he showed her where the bathroom was, then walked her into a bedroom.

"Do you remember what bag you packed your pajamas in?" he asked, setting her on the bed.

"My carryon, I think."

"Okay. Sit tight."

Once he was gone, Kim flopped over onto the plump feather pillow, too tired even to lift her feet off the floor.

When Mark returned, she was almost asleep. Through her lashes she saw him set down her bags and tiptoe to the bed. He looked down at her, chewing on his lower lip in a manner that made him look charmingly boyish. In his hands were her old flannel pajamas. He looked from her to them and back to her again.

"Kim, you've got me over a barrel." He spoke quietly, more to himself than to her. "Ah, well." He tossed the pajamas aside, then lifted her legs onto the bed and covered her with a comforter. "Good night," he whispered, pressing a hand to her head. "See you in the morning."

When the door closed, Kim put her hand where his had been and imagined she still felt the warmth. Sleep was stealing over her fast, and her thoughts were becoming muddled. She knew Mark had been kind only because she'd fainted. Otherwise, he would have bundled her off to this room as brusquely as he'd rushed her through the airport. And why not? They were nothing to each other but strangers, strangers haphazardly linked through a common relative.

Still, it was a relief to be cocooned in this soft bed so far from home. And that hand to her head... People needed touches like that. She knew. She'd gone a lifetime without them. This... this was nice, she thought, curling up her legs. She would soak up the rest, pretend the peace was real and lasting—and continue the battle tomorrow.

MARK PICKED UP the phone, scowled at it a full minute, then put it down again. It would be after midnight back East and Miriam would probably be asleep. He made himself a drink instead, a vodka and tonic, double. Then, drink in hand, he wandered through the downstairs rooms, unsettled and awake.

He still had work to do, but he knew he'd never concentrate. When he'd seen Kim slump to the floor, he'd sworn his heart had stopped. In his care less than an hour, and already she was dying on him! Guilt had swamped him immediately. He might dislike her being here but he didn't have to make the fact so obvious!

She was such a tiny thing. Thin, light in his arms, too light for her height, which had to be five foot six or seven. And so pale.

He paced down the hall to the foyer, stopping to gaze into the living room. When he noticed her vinyl coat and boots, he laughed dryly.

She wasn't really bad looking, once you got a good look at her. Basically she had nice features: long thick hair the color of dark copper; big wide-set eyes that amazingly were the very same shade of red brown; and a mouth that, well, he preferred not to think about her mouth. The term "bee-stung" kept buzzing round his head for some reason, and if ever the term fit...

But the fact remained, the girl hadn't the vaguest idea how to play up those features, or how to dress. One look at

her and the word "underprivileged" immediately flashed
across one's mind, and he was beginning to worry again
about his party. What would he do with her if she was still
here?

Mark stared at his drink, a frown tightening his brow. She
wasn't quite what he'd expected. Granted, she had an edge,
but not the sharp aggressive edge of someone who'd grown
up in an inner city. Her edge was more defensive, quiet, like
a barbed-wire fence thrown up to keep things out. And in
her eyes, he'd glimpsed a vulnerability Miriam hadn't prepared him for. That vulnerability, that little-girl-lost look—
he didn't think it was an act. As they'd watched TV, he'd
caught her twirling her hair round and round her finger. But
the worst part was he'd suffered an urge to put his arm
around her to calm the nervous habit.

He took a sip from his glass. Something else was bothering him. She seemed older than he'd expected. Not that she
looked old; she just had a maturity about her that was puzzling.

Mark swirled his drink. He had to nip this curiosity in the
bud. It was the first stage of getting involved.

Kim's purse, a shapeless brown satchel, was lying under
the coffee table. Mark looked at it a long while, fighting a
gnawing in his gut. Finally he hauled it off the floor. But his
drink was nearly gone before he'd eased his conscience
enough to throw back the flap.

It was her wallet he wanted to find. Just that. But to get
to the wallet, he first had to remove a few plastic makeup
cases, a brush, comb and, curiously, a book entitled *Childhood Diseases; Diagnoses and Treatment*. Mark stared at
the book, frowning fiercely. Beneath this was a thick black
tube he recognized as Mace. Defense or weapon? he wondered fleetingly. Under that was a full change of under-
wear. Sturdy white cotton, he noted with surprise.

Finally, her wallet. He snapped it open and, holding his
breath, went looking for I.D. Much to his surprise, he found

a driver's license. A second later he let fly a whispered curse. The girl was twenty-two years old! Actually she'd be twenty-three next month, three days before his own birthday, he calculated quickly. Twenty-three!

He meant to close the wallet then—it was the right thing to do—but it seemed to burn in his hand. With a vague sense of recklessness, he flipped the plastic window containing her license and checked out her medical insurance card. Coverage had expired a year ago. Damn, what was the matter with her? Nobody could live without insurance these days. Stuffed into the next window was a library card so used that some of its print was unreadable. His frown was beginning to hurt.

He went through all the windows, expecting the usual assortment of Visa and MasterCards, but it seemed the girl didn't even have an account at Sears.

In the money pocket he counted $218. He lowered the wallet to his lap and gazed abstractedly across the room. He couldn't imagine traveling two thousand miles to embark on a new life with a measly two hundred bucks and no credit cards. Perhaps—perhaps she'd divided her money and hidden the rest in her luggage.

As he replaced the wallet, something else caught his eye at the bottom of the bag—a small spiral notebook. Only after he'd opened it and read "Sept. 28. Went to the movies tonight..." did he realize it was a diary. He clapped it shut immediately. Some lines he would not cross.

He stuffed everything back into the bag and held it against him, his arms folded loosely on top. Who the hell *was* that girl sleeping upstairs in his spare room? And more to the point, what was he going to do with her until Miriam got here?

CHAPTER THREE

WAS IT MORNING already? Kim didn't want to wake up, didn't want to face the fact that she was in Colorado and not New York. Reluctantly she lifted aside a silky comforter and swung her feet to the floor.

Sunlight was pouring through the windows whose shades Mark had forgotten to pull last night, brightening a room that looked freshly painted, a fragile cream tone that blended softly with the mauve carpeting and draperies. The furniture was small-scaled French provincial, feminine and light, the sort of furniture a man would choose for a young girl, she reflected.

Her thoughts returned to Mark, his concern and gentle care last evening. Being pampered had felt wonderful, even if it hadn't come from the heart.

She smiled at her pajamas, tossed on a nearby chair. He'd looked so confounded, standing by her bed with them in his hand. Confounded and incredibly handsome. Kim groaned, closing her eyes to shut out the image. Those thoughts had to end right now.

She got to her feet and opened her suitcase. Last evening at the airport, the idea of returning home had seemed so appealing. It was obvious that Miriam had thrust her into Mark's life and that he wasn't pleased by the arrangement. But this morning, the idea of all that money wasted on airfare struck her as absurd. Absurd and foolhardy. Miriam would throw a fit if Kim showed up back on her doorstep.

She had to stick to the itinerary as planned. If she got busy right away, as Mark hoped she would, perhaps she'd find a job and a suitable apartment and be out of here in a few days.

Kim hadn't anticipated the need to rush these decisions. She'd assumed her stepmother would want to give the final okay to any apartment she found. Otherwise Miriam would've entrusted her with a security deposit.

Now Miriam would just have to trust her judgment. Kim would call and ask her to wire the necessary money. And in the meantime she supposed she could endure Mark Johnson a few more days. Besides, after last night, she didn't find the prospect all that unpleasant.

Robe in hand, Kim hurried across the hall to the bathroom. On the way she noticed Mark's bedroom door was open, the bed neatly made. Had he already left for work? she wondered. Did he work on Saturday?

After a long hot shower and thorough shampoo she felt immeasurably better. She looked better, too, she decided, examining herself in the dresser mirror. She slipped into fresh jeans, a pink mohair sweater that warmed her clear scrubbed complexion, and brushed her long hair into a loose topknot that gave her a soft Gibson-girl look. The style also hid the limp broken ends of her hair.

She could hear voices rising from below. Evidently Mark was still home. She decided to put on a touch of makeup.

While fastening her watch, she realized she was trembling. Why she should be jittery about facing Mark Johnson again was beyond her. So what if he happened to be the sort of man women habitually swooned over? She was hardly the swooning type. She closed her suitcase, smoothed her sweater and quietly opened the door.

The night before she'd been too tired to notice any of the details of the house. Now she realized there were two staircases leading up to the second floor, the wide carpeted one she'd climbed last night and another, a plain boxed-in affair at the back of the hall. The voices were rising from this well. From the kitchen, she guessed. She recognized Mark's warm deep rumble, but the other voice was quite feminine—smooth, silken, cultured.

"So, when am I going to meet this little ward of yours?" the woman asked. Her laugh was a low seductive tease.

Kim snapped to when she realized *she* was the topic of conversation. She eased down the narrow wooden steps, her sneakers making no sound. She stopped halfway and sat.

"I told you, she isn't my ward, Suzanne. Can't I get you more coffee? A Danish? Maybe a mouth gag?"

"You're keeping something from me, aren't you, you devil?" The woman laughed again.

"Don't you have somewhere to go?"

"Yes, upstairs to drag that little girl out of bed to see what you're hiding."

From the scuffling sounds that followed, Kim imagined the woman had pretended to rise and Mark was trying to stop her. Both of them were laughing. Kim hugged her knees and rested her chin on them, feeling an unexpected pang of loneliness. Mark's guest was obviously a special friend.

"I'm sure she'll be down any minute," he said. "I heard the shower running a while ago. And she isn't exactly a little girl, Suzanne," he added hesitantly. "She's . . . she's just a few weeks shy of twenty-three."

"Are you kidding me!" This time the woman's voice was devoid of teasing.

"I wish. I checked out her driver's license last night."

Kim sat bolt upright. Mark had gone through her purse? She was shocked—and then in a matter of seconds, furious.

"Maybe my sister said something and I didn't hear, but I swear, Sue, I really thought she was a teenager."

"Good Lord! You have a twenty-three-year-old woman living with you!"

"Keep your voice down. Twenty-three is still awfully young. Besides, it's only for a couple of weeks."

"The world was created in less time, love."

"Will you knock it off! Wait till you see her."

Kim's back straightened even further, her breathing arrested.

"She's just a kid, and one who needs a lot of help. In fact, I was hoping you'd give me a hand with her."

"You've got me more curious than ever. What's the matter with her?"

Yes, what? Kim pleaded.

"Let's just say she could use some polish. Makeup, clothing, that sort of thing."

"That all?"

"Yes, unless you can do something with her Brooklyn accent."

Kim closed her eyes, remembering Miriam's taunts about her delusions of fitting in among higher-class people. Kim hadn't believed her. She'd thought she looked and behaved and sounded just fine. But apparently Miriam was right!

Kim became aware of a meditative silence. Then, "That's surface, Mark. What does she need underneath?"

She waited, straining her ears, but Mark didn't reply.

"Hey." The woman's voice dropped to a serious register. "Do I detect a look of concern in those big baby-blues?"

"Of course not. I told you I don't have time to get involved with that girl. I'm only doing this out of a sense of duty to my sister."

"Good. You had me scared for a sec. Thought the city's most exciting bachelor was going mellow on me."

"Hardly. If I had my way, she wouldn't be here at all."

Huddled on the stairs, Kim fought a stinging in her eyes. So, last evening's kindness *had* been an act, just as she'd suspected. Well, Mr. Johnson needn't worry. She'd be hanged if she stayed under his roof another night!

"I've simply been concerned about the party next weekend," he continued, "and, well, what she'll wear, for instance."

"You're going to have her at your party?" The woman sounded horrified.

"I know, but I can't very well lock her in her room."

"And how do you propose to explain her to Father and the two other stuffed shirts you work for?"

"Suzanne!" Mark's voice rose in frustration. "There's nothing to explain. She's a kid. She's my niece."

"Stepniece," the woman corrected.

Mark grumbled. "So far, you're the only person who knows that, and if you don't mind, I'd like to keep it that way."

Kim had heard enough. Although part of her longed to creep back upstairs and hide beneath the comforter, her anger won out over her pain and she stomped down the stairs, instead.

Mark was lifting a mug to his lips when he noticed her. The mug halted in midjourney and his whole body went still. Only his eyes seemed capable of movement as they took a slow, slightly startled survey of her, ending as they had begun, with her upswept hair. She noticed him swallow hard.

Good. She hoped he felt guilty as sin, realizing she'd overheard his cruel remarks. She lifted her chin and returned a cool aloof stare.

The woman sitting at the table with him turned, her shimmering blond hair swinging across her shoulders. She was as beautiful as her voice had promised. When she saw Kim, her green eyes widened and her smile wilted.

Mark cleared his throat. "Well, aren't you looking, uh, rested this morning?" He got to his feet, bumping his chair back awkwardly. "Suzanne, this is..." He hesitated. Had he forgotten her name already? "Kim. Kim, this is Suzanne Brightman, a friend of mine."

"Darling, I believe the term these days is 'significant other,'" Suzanne teased.

Kim got the distinct impression the comment was made for her edification, not Mark's. She extended her hand and forced herself to smile. "Pleased to meet you."

"Hello, Kim. Welcome to Colorado Springs." It was a restrained welcome.

"Thank you. Is there any more coffee, Mark?"

He stared at her as if she'd asked him to solve a complex algebra equation. "Uh, yes. I have orange juice, too."

"Coffee's fine."

"But not as good for you as juice." He seemed determined to treat her like a ten-year-old.

"Is there a diner nearby?" she asked pointedly.

His lips twitched, point taken. "The pot's on the counter, mugs overhead."

"How long will you be here before your mother joins you, Kim?" Suzanne inquired.

Kim glanced up from the pot. She'd be gone just as soon as she could pack, but that was a secret best kept to herself. "I'm not sure. It depends on how quickly she can sell our house."

"Well, I hope you don't get too lonely or bored. Mark's so busy these days..."

"Yes, he's told me." *Over and over.* "I'm quite used to keeping my own company, thanks." Kim leaned against the counter and took solace in her steaming coffee.

"What do you do for a living, Kim?"

"I...work. What do you do?" She hadn't meant to sound snide. She'd only wanted to be vague and shift attention away from herself. But from the way Mark was choking, she guessed she'd really messed up.

"I'm an attorney," Suzanne replied frostily.

"Really?" She would've sworn Suzanne spent all her time shopping and doing her nails. "That's wonderful!"

Suzanne ignored her compliment and got to her feet. "Sorry I can't stay longer, Mark, but I'm meeting those water-rights people in fifteen minutes."

Mark helped her on with her cape, a rich red wool that matched her lipstick and nails perfectly. "Maybe next Saturday you two'll have a better chance to become acquainted."

Suzanne smiled noncommittally.

Mark followed her to the kitchen door. Out on the step she turned and, making only a minimal effort to lower her voice, said, "I see what you mean about her, Mark. I wish I could help but..." She wagged her head as if to say he was saddled with a hopeless case. As angry as Kim was, the comment still managed to hurt.

Suzanne then wrapped one hand around Mark's neck to draw him down into a kiss. Kim looked away, feeling an oddly piercing disappointment.

Only after Suzanne drove off did Mark turn. He cleared his throat, hitched a shoulder and moved to the table. With tight jerky movements he cleared away mugs, spoons, napkins, the newspaper, his eyes trained on his task as if looking up might turn him to stone. "Have a seat," he said.

Kim sat, carefully placing her mug on the table. Mark's eyes fixed on the mug. Then slowly he let them follow the curling steam up, over her soft pink sweater, along the column of her neck, to her face. Something in his expression made her heart take an erratic leap.

Abruptly he hurried to the sink. "How's your dizziness today?" He turned on the tap and scrubbed a frying pan too vigorously.

"It comes and goes."

"Well, hang in. It won't last long." He was wearing black dress shoes, charcoal trousers, a crisp pearl-gray shirt, maroon tie and trendy suspenders. Kim's eyes traveled furtively, taking in the details. She'd never met anyone who could look so businesslike and yet exude such sex appeal.

She shook her head to knock away the nonsense. "Does Suzanne work for her father, too?"

"How did you know I..." He paused, swallowed. "Uh, yes."

"Cozy."

"What?"

"Dating long?"

Frowning, he opened the dishwasher and put a few things inside. "A few months. And we really aren't serious. She was kidding about that 'significant other' stuff."

Kim doubted that.

Mark refilled his coffee mug and sat opposite her. "Listen, I wanted to take the whole day off, to help you settle in, but there's just too much to do. If all goes well, though, I may be home early. Twelve, one o'clock."

Kim glanced at her watch. It was already quarter to nine. "Don't rush on my account." She needed the time alone to pack and get out. "So, what's happening next Saturday night?"

"I have about forty people coming over."

"For dinner?"

"Good Lord, no. Just a party."

"Oh. That should be fun."

"You'd think." He shook his head ever so slightly, like a man in regret.

Kim looked aside, her jaw hardening. "If you're worried about me crashing it..."

"Oh, no. That never occurred—"

She pinned him with a knowing stare. "I don't expect to be included. I don't know any of your friends."

Mark blew out a long disgruntled breath. "Kim, stop. It's not you." But he didn't meet her gaze. "If I sound unenthusiastic, it's only because I don't feel ready to have people over. This house isn't ready."

Kim made a quick sweep of the kitchen. Like the living room and her bedroom, the kitchen could've been featured in a home-decorating magazine.

"Never mind," he said. "It's not for you to worry. I've hired a good caterer and stocked enough liquor to float a navy. Maybe that'll be enough to carry the affair."

"I'm sure you'll do fine." Kim resented his flimsy excuses. How dumb did he think she was?

They fell silent, Kim studying a patch of sunlight on the table, Mark studying Kim. She could feel his scrutiny as palpably as if he was touching her. Her cheeks warmed as she wondered what pitiful thing he saw. Leaving here would be a relief in more ways than one. She'd never encountered anyone who made her feel so self-conscious.

"Well, Kimberly, I have to be leaving. While I'm gone, please make yourself a good breakfast. After that, I imagine you'll want to unpack. I'm really sorry I have to go, but when I get back, maybe we can go see that real-estate guy together."

Kim stared at the ceiling. "Yeah, sure." She didn't need his real-estate guy. She didn't need any of Mark's grudging favors.

He hauled himself out of his chair, pulled on a sports jacket that accentuated his athletic build, picked up his briefcase and walked to the back door. There he paused, his gaze sliding over her again. "By the way, you look...rested today," he finished, falling back on the same word he'd chosen earlier. Kim smiled ruefully. "Rested" was probably the kindest word he could find.

As soon as he was gone, she hurried from the kitchen in search of a phone. The very first room she ran into contained a large desk and, bingo, the object of her search. For a moment, however, altitude sickness overtook her, and she had to cling to the desk to regain her balance. While she stood there, her gaze lifted and swept the room.

Apparently this was Mark's study. Besides the desk, the room contained a leather recliner, a brass bridge lamp and several stacks of books and files. Yet overhead hung an absolutely lovely chandelier, its crystal prisms dusty with neglect, and on the far wall, flanking a deep bay window, were two delicately milled cabinets that should've been filled with china, instead of books. This should be a dining room! Kim realized in astonishment. And almost immediately another realization hit her. Mark had not been making excuses. His house, or at least this room, *wasn't* ready for entertaining.

But she couldn't think about that now. She found a phone book in one of the desk drawers and, hands shaking, flipped it open. First she called a local women's shelter to see about bunking in there for a while. Then she called the YWCA and a youth hostel, just for added insurance. When she finished her calls, she felt more confident. She was going to get by. She didn't need to stay in this house where she was a grudging responsibility, among people to whom she was an embarrassment, with a man who distrusted her to the point of ransacking her personal belongings.

Of course, explaining the move to Miriam wouldn't be easy, but she'd worry about that later. Right now what she had to do was pack and get out. Mark hadn't much liked the idea of her flying back East last evening, and she was sure he wouldn't care for her moving into a shelter any better.

She was about to get up when her gaze fell on a framed snapshot sitting on the desk. Her stomach clenched as she recognized her stepmother. But this Miriam wasn't quite the harridan she knew. Kim frowned in puzzlement. And Mark—how young and eager! The two were smiling, and deep affection shone in their eyes.

Kim let her gaze sweep the rest of the desk's neat clutter. A tower of ponderous law books, topped by a volume of "Calvin and Hobbes" comic strips. An appointment calendar, solidly filled in. A pipe wrench. A dog-eared paperback entitled *Financial Security: A Plan for Life*. A vase with two daffodils. A ceramic mug, embossed with a decal of a basketball and inscribed with a dozen boys' wobbly signatures. "Thanks for a great year, Coach," she read among the names.

Kim barely breathed, wondering who Mark Johnson really was. She also wondered why the prospect of never finding out was suddenly bothering her.

Damn! It wasn't worth puzzling over. She got to her feet and dashed for the stairs.

Ten minutes later she dashed back down and dropped her bags by the front door. Morning sunshine illuminated more rooms she hadn't noticed last night—a large formal parlor across the foyer, a sun porch beyond and a large alcove that would make a fine study. All three rooms were empty, except for a shroud of dust and neglect. Mark's party situation was worse than she'd thought.

But that was *his* problem, she reminded herself, heading for the study. There she phoned for a cab. Satisfied she'd soon be on her way, Kim breathed a sigh of relief.

She hadn't taken two steps down the hall, however, when the front door opened and Mark strolled in, nearly toppling over her mound of luggage.

Kim's heart dropped to her ankles. "What are you doing here?" she squeaked.

He gave her one searching look, and she knew he'd guessed what she was up to. He flung his jacket across the foyer, swearing under his breath.

"You can't make me stay." Kim pointed a shaky finger at him. "I'm over twenty-one. I can do as I please."

Mark rubbed the back of his neck. "After the wrangling I did to get out early, I ought to throttle you." Instead, he opened the door wide and said, "Fine. I don't care. Go."

Kim was stunned. She swallowed hard, then moved forward. "You mean it?"

"Yes. Go. Door's open."

Kim picked up her coat and slipped one arm into it. "I hope you're not angry."

"Me? Angry? Why should I be angry? Because I'm up for a promotion and can't afford to be taking time off like this? Because you'd rather be hanging out on some street corner, instead of taking advantage of the opportunity Miriam's offering you? Gee, I must be crazy to be angry!"

"Hanging out on a street corner?" Kim eyed him incredulously. "Sorry, but I'm more convinced than ever that I should leave. I don't belong here." She didn't belong anywhere. "The sooner I go, the sooner you can get your precious life back to normal." A car horn tooted outside. "That must be my taxi."

She was nearly by him when he gripped her arm. "Wait. I can't let you do this, Kim. I made a promise to Miriam."

"And I'm relieving you of it." She yanked free of his hold and stepped outside.

"Answer one question, Kim. What's so important in New York that you can't wait to get back? Is it a young man? Is it friends? Drugs?"

Kim half turned. "New York? Sorry to disappoint you, but I'm only going as far as the nearest women's shelter."

His expression clouded. "I don't understand. Why are you doing this?"

She shook her head, hopeless of ever making him see. "Gotta go."

"Kim." The urgency that thickened his voice made her stop. "Does this have anything to do with the conversation I was having with Suzanne when you came downstairs?"

For a moment, her throat tightened. "Maybe." It didn't make sense that this man should matter so much so soon. "Look, Mark, I don't want to be here any more than you want me here and, believe me, I wouldn't have come if it hadn't been for those plane tickets Miriam bought. I never intended to be a burden to you. I'm used to doing for myself. But evidently just my presence here is a problem, so I'll leave. It's that simple."

He looked uneasy. "This won't go over well with Miriam."

"Don't worry about Miriam. I'll call her tonight."

"But..."

Kim waved and walked on toward the waiting taxi.

The driver was already stowing her bags in the back seat when Mark called to her. "Kim, I'm sorry." Her heart took an erratic lurch. Although she hadn't known him long, she was sure he didn't apologize often.

The taxi didn't even reach the corner when doubt began to assail her. What was she doing running to a shelter when she had wonderful accommodations here? The thought of sleeping shoulder to shoulder with strangers made her skin crawl. But more than anything, it was Mark who shook her resolve. He confused her, probably because he was confused himself. He didn't seem to know whether he welcomed her or not.

Well, if she did return, it wouldn't be with the childish expectations she'd flown here with. She'd withdraw into herself, shift into emotional neutrality and thereby avoid any further pain of rejection.

Feeling rather foolish, Kim leaned forward and told the driver to turn back. A few minutes later she was knocking on Mark's front door, her heart racing.

Much too quickly the door opened. She pulled in a deep breath of courage, lifted her chin and stated, "I gave what you said some thought, and I've decided to stay."

Mark smiled, a flash of relief, and then wiped his hand over his mouth to erase the expression. "Come on. Let's take these up to your room and unpack." He gripped her suitcase and turned.

"Just a minute. If I'm going to stay, we have to get a few things cleared up."

"Oh?" He paused on the stairs.

"Mark, I..." She looked at the wallpaper rather than meet his eyes. "I'm sorry I've been so emotional. This move is a big step for me. I've worried about it for weeks, unsure if it's right."

Mark put down her bag, studying her thoughtfully. "I suppose I've been running on overdrive myself. Tense about my job. Tense about living with someone. I've never done that before, and I guess my fears of what you'd do to my life swelled all out of proportion."

Kim nodded, accepting his reasoning and the apology implied within it. "I think my nerves have settled somewhat..."

"And you won't be trying to leave again?"

She shook her head. "And I hope you'll believe me when I say you don't have to entertain me or keep me busy or even talk to me. And I don't expect to hobnob with your friends."

Mark looked aside, fidgeting with his tie.

"What I want is exactly the opposite—to be left alone, as if I were a stranger, because really that's all I am to you. I just want to room here, and I want the opportunity to get a job and work."

Mark's head pulled back. "At what?"

"At anything. It doesn't matter. I just need to work, and here comes the hitch—I want to save the money I make."

Mark looked thoroughly confused now.

"What I'm asking is, will you be kind enough not to charge me room and board? In compensation, I'll clean and do your laundry, and I was thinking you could use some help getting the house ready for your party."

"Good Lord, Kim. You're a guest here. I never intended to charge you, and you needn't feel you have to repay me."

She shook her head vigorously. "No. No favors. I want to be treated like someone you've rented a room to, okay?"

"But...*why?*"

"Because business relationships are easy. You know exactly what to expect from them, and what not to expect—that especially."

She watched her meaning find its mark. He blinked, looked aside and swallowed.

"It isn't your fault. I was the one who flew out here looking for an uncle. It was unfair to you—and pretty darn stupid of me. But all that's worked out of my system now."

Mark lowered himself to the carpeted stairs and tapped his fingertips in somber thought. "So, what are you saving your money for?" he finally asked.

She stared at the floor, twirling a strand of hair that had come loose from her topknot. A dozen uncertainties weighed on her heart, a dozen possible turns of fate she needed to prepare for.

"Are you in trouble, Kim?"

"In trouble?" She noticed Mark's color deepen. "You mean . . . pregnant?" Astonished, she laughed. "Of course not."

"Then what?"

Kim thought about an apartment and rent, groceries and school bills. But mostly she thought about Theodore and Miriam shutting her out of their life. It was a black vision that wasn't likely to happen. Still, the vision persisted. "Let's just leave it. I have my reasons, okay?"

Mark blew out a long slow breath. "Okay, Kimberly. We'll do it your way. I have no problem with your getting a job. That was the game plan, anyway. Now, do you want any help looking?"

"No. Just the newspaper and maybe a bus schedule. I have three letters of recommendation from past employers and lots of experience. I'll get by."

Mark shook his head. "I've never seen such bullheaded independence." He leaned back on the stairs, staring at her narrowly. "You have a driver's license, don't you?"

She chewed the inside of her cheek. They both knew darn well she did. "Yes."

"How come? Given the congestion in New York, the auto theft, the subway system—"

"No reason. One of the salesmen on the car lot where I worked taught me how to drive. Slow days, he'd take me out, different cars every time. He wanted to keep the batteries alive more than anything else." That wasn't entirely the truth. Tom had been interested in her romantically, too, an interest she hadn't reciprocated.

"Do you know how to drive a stick shift?"

Kim eyed him guardedly. "Why?"

"I have two vehicles. You can take my Cherokee. It's a hell of a lot easier than trying to catch buses."

Take his Cherokee? Kim walked to the door and stared out its beveled window. She heard Mark get off the stairs and cross the foyer.

"You'd do that?" She turned, nearly bumping into him.

"Do what?"

"Let me borrow your car?"

"Sure. Why not?"

Kim studied his handsome face, searching for signs of a secret agenda. "No, Mark. The question is *why.*"

His smile faded. "Why? Why would I let you take my car?" He stared at her awhile, then blinked like a blind man receiving sight. "Oh, Lord, Kim, hasn't anybody ever *helped* you before?"

She looked everywhere but at him. "I'd better go unpack." Before he could protest, she hurried for the stairs.

KIM'S CLOTHING barely filled half the dresser, and the few things she hung in the closet looked lost. Most of her wardrobe was back in New York, along with a lifetime of accumulated personal possessions. She'd packed everything before leaving, trusting Miriam to ship the boxes later with the furniture. Now she wished she'd brought a few more outfits with her.

She studied her reflection in the dresser mirror, recalling Mark's hurtful comments about her appearance. Did she really look so bad? While her clothing wasn't new or costly, it wasn't offensive, either. Jeans. A sweater. She looked about as ordinary as a person could get.

Ordinary. That certainty wasn't the word to describe Suzanne, Kim thought in dismay.

She leaned closer, examining the mascara and blush she'd stroked on this morning. She could hardly see it, and suddenly a vision of Suzanne superimposed itself on her washed-out face. Suzanne had probably applied more kinds of makeup than Kim knew what to do with, and the effect had been riveting. Her hair had been beautiful, too—rich, pampered satin.

Kim removed the pins from her topknot and finger-combed her long frizzled waves. Her hair was a wreck, but was it an irrevocable wreck? she wondered. If she found a really good hairdresser...

A knock at her door startled her. "Kim?"

What did Mark want now? She'd thought he understood. Detachment. Noninvolvement. No favors or obligations and, hence, no unmet expectations.

Hastily she repinned her hair and opened the door.

"Hi. I brought up today's newspaper, if you want to look through the job ads."

Her gaze flicked from his chest to his face in quick shy forays. He'd changed from his suit into jeans and a black sweater, looking ruggedly casual and very masculine.

"Thanks." She took the paper without a smile. This wasn't a favor, and she wasn't feeling gratitude. She wasn't.

"Kim, how about taking a break? I took the afternoon off to be with you. How about if we go for a drive?"

"Thanks, but I'm not interested in sight-seeing. Use the free time for yourself." She closed the door even as he was framing a protest. From the other side she heard a growled mutter and then his heavy footsteps on the stairs.

She sat and read the job ads, and when she was done, she got up and paced her room. Downstairs a whole lot of banging was going on. Whatever Mark had decided to do, it certainly was noisy.

She picked up the paper and, still pacing, reread the items she'd circled. If only she had access to a typewriter, she could get started writing letters.

She hated to bother Mark, but on the other hand, he'd come to her door willing to be bothered—he, who'd professed to have no time to get involved—and she had turned him away. Poor man. She'd put him on an emotional seesaw. But that was only because she was on one herself.

But no more. If they were to coexist like two rational adults instead of sulky children, it was time she evened out. She was sure she could be polite and still manage to stay detached.

"Hi," she said, peeking into the parlor.

Mark was standing on a ladder, unscrewing the corroded drapery hardware from one of the windows. "Hello." His voice was as dry as dust.

"I have a favor to ask. Do you have a typewriter I can borrow?"

"In there." He tipped his head toward the dining room.

"Thanks. What are you doing?"

"Something I should've done a long time ago. Hand me that pair of pliers, will you?"

Kim crossed the empty room, her sneakers squeaking on the hardwood floor. "Here ya go."

He didn't look at her. His profile remained peevish.

"Mark, I offered to help and I meant it. I realize you're in a fix, with only a week till the party and all."

"Here." He handed back the pliers, his face as expressionless as stone.

"I-Is there something I can do?"

"Not unless you know how to turn this house into a home in one week, the home of an attorney you'd trust with your life, or at least with your ten-million-dollar business." He swore as the screwdriver he was using slipped. "An attorney," he grunted, "of tremendous intelligence, taste, power. Oh, power's way up there on the list."

Kim cast a disparaging look at the room. "No problem. Where's my magic wand."

He finally got the hardware free and moved the ladder to the next window. As he climbed the rungs, his head glanced the old window shade, and suddenly the whole thing—shade, heavy wood roller and years of dust—came tumbling down on top of him. He let fly a string of swearwords as he flailed his arm against the brittle skein of unwinding canvas.

"Mark, are you all right?" Kim ran toward the ladder.

As the mess settled to the floor, he winced and rubbed his head. "Ow!"

She couldn't help grinning.

"It isn't funny."

"Of course it isn't." With an effort, she sobered her expression.

Mark clambered down the ladder and brushed the dust off his sweater. On the floor behind him, the spring within the shade roller suddenly popped and whirred, the contraption's last dying gasp. Kim could see he was trying to ignore the sound, but the edges of his scowl were crumbling, and when he turned his head aside, she was sure it was to conceal a smile.

"What exactly do you hope to do with this room before Saturday?"

"Make it look presentable, that's all. There isn't enough time to do it right, the way I intend to eventually."

"Was the whole house like this when you bought it?"

"Uh-huh. I've worked at it when I could, did the rooms I thought were essential first. Unfortunately these are still on the waiting list." He sat against a windowsill, fascinated, it seemed, by her hair. Kim wondered if something was caught in it.

"You do the work yourself?"

"Yes. And don't get on my back the way Suzanne does. I realize the whole place could be finished by now if I'd just hire someone, but I like working with my hands. It's... therapeutic."

Kim looked at him calmly. "You don't have to explain yourself to me."

"Oh. Oh, well, good."

She walked away from his puzzled gaze. "I see what you mean, though, about not having time for the full face-lift, especially if you plan to fix up the dining room, too. Do you?"

"Yes. Any ideas?"

"Aside from canceling the party?"

He pinned her with a stare, not at all amused.

"Well, after you finish wrestling with the shades, I could wash the windows. And the walls. I bet a quick wash would make them look a lot better. But there is one problem, Mark."

"What's that?" His mood appeared to be lightening.

"Furniture. You don't have any."

"Hmm." Slowly he walked the perimeter of the room. "How about if I move the kitchen table into the dining room, scatter the living-room set here and there...? No? You're shaking your head, no?"

Kim bit her lip to keep from laughing. Mark had a certain Puckish charm she hadn't been aware of.

"Oh, well." He threw up his hands. "I didn't think it was such a hot idea myself."

Kim stroked the mahogany fireplace mantel. "This is really a beautiful house."

"I know. That's why I bought it."

She turned. "That all?" Gazing at the bay window that faced the street, she could almost see the twinkling lights of a Christmas tree, smell the scent of pine . . .

"What do you mean, that all?"

She shrugged. "It's such a family house. I was just wondering if you planned to . . . to fill it someday."

"I've never given it much thought," he said too quickly.

Heat pooled in Kim's cheeks. How had she let herself wander into such personal territory? Best to get back to the matter at hand.

"This party—it obviously means a lot to you."

He shrugged. "I guess."

"Who's going to be here? Your boss?"

"Yes, and there are three of them. Their wives, my colleagues, business associates, clients . . ."

"Ah. I'm getting the picture. And is your promotion riding on how well you perform?" She was afraid sarcasm slipped into her voice.

Mark's brow lowered. "Of course not. Where'd you get an idea like that? My work's good, Kim. I'm careful, thorough. They'll judge me on those merits."

"Of course." But from the way Mark was scowling at the floor, arms folded tight across his broad chest, Kim still sensed that *something* was hanging in the balance.

With his attention momentarily diverted, she let her eyes travel the length of him, from his thick sun-dusted brown hair to his long muscle-corded legs, defined by well-worn jeans.

Feeling a sudden uncomfortable heat, she glanced away. Good heavens, what was the matter with her? If she started paying attention to how attractive Mark was, living with him would soon become an agony of complications.

She cleared her throat. "Have you thought about renting furniture?"

Mark uncrossed his arms in surprise. "No."

''Well, you obviously need more, but I wouldn't suggest going out and buying it. You're too much in a rush.''

''It's worth a shot.''

''I think it's your only shot.''

Mark nodded, his smile broadening with assurance. ''Then it's settled. Grab your coat and we'll be off.''

''We?''

Yes. You offered to help, didn't you?''

Kim told herself she was only acting as an uninvolved stranger, as a polite boarder who was breezing through Mark's life, and that the real Kim Wade was safely crouched somewhere deep and tight within. But as she dashed past the hall mirror on the way to the front door, she noticed her eyes were suspiciously bright and she knew that the bloom in her cheeks had nothing at all to do with detachment.

CHAPTER FOUR

MARK DIDN'T KNOW what to make of himself, walking along by Kim's side through the rental store. Usually he was fairly even keeled, but since her arrival, he'd been riding an emotional roller coaster.

Just an hour ago he'd thought he was mad at her. He'd thought her idea of their treating each other like strangers was great. He neither wanted nor needed Kim Wade in his life.

Yet, no sooner had she closeted herself in her room than their policy of noninvolvement had begun to bother him. Then, after she'd suggested renting furniture, he hadn't just invited her to come along; he'd insisted on it. He might've chalked up his actions to his sense of duty toward Miriam; he was merely giving Kim something "involving" to do, as Miriam had requested. But that didn't explain why he was having such a good time in the process.

If Mark didn't understand himself, he made even less sense of Kim. The longer he spent in her company the more curious he grew. She wandered through the cluttered warehouse, close by his side, amazed by the array of furnishings they could rent.

"This place is great," she whispered. He liked the way she leaned in, as if sharing a confidence. "Oh, look, even paintings. Do you think we can rent a few paintings?"

She was like a child, wide-eyed, shy, enthusiastic—but a child who knew the difference between Hepplewhite and

Sheridan, neither of which she recommended because they were too formal.

"Where'd you learn so much about decorating?"

"I don't know anything about decorating." She laughed as if the idea was absurd. "I just read magazines like everybody else."

"You like to read, don't you?"

"Mmm. Oh, Mark, look at that wicker set. Would you like to do the sun porch, too?"

Her cheeks had warmed, her brown eyes sparkled, and when she smiled she seemed to glow from within. She was prettier than he'd thought, Mark realized, studying her from behind a large cloisonné urn. Her shiny black coat still left a lot to be desired, but that wasn't her fault. Her clothes were inexpensive, and inexpensive just meant you didn't have money for anything better. He understood. All too well.

She suddenly became aware of his scrutiny, and her smile faded. "What? What?" she asked defensively.

"Nothing."

"I'm taking over, aren't I? Sorry. It's your house, your party..."

"No, it's quite all right. You're just being yourself, and I think I like it."

As soon as the words were out, Mark knew he'd blundered. Not only had he crossed the line of noninvolvement, but he'd reminded Kim that she had, too. She frowned, then closed up like a flower at sunset and remained that way the rest of their shopping trip.

Ah, well. Maybe she was being the smart one here. No matter how strongly Miriam wanted her to sink roots, he doubted she'd stick around Colorado Springs for long. Why else would she settle for just any job, instead of going through a career counselor? And why not tell him what she was saving for? No, this girl had travel in her eyes, and he'd better maintain a safe distance or he might get too attached.

Out in the parking lot, he opened the car door for her. "That was kind of fun, wasn't it?"

Kim slipped in without meeting his eyes. "Yes. The house'll be filled, right down to potted palms. You should be pleased." She almost looked angry.

"Thanks for the idea."

She shrugged and sank further into herself. Mark drummed his fingers on the steering wheel. Her silences were driving him batty. She reminded him of a pond, calm on the surface but swirling with currents beneath. He wished he knew what made her so prickly and yet put such vulnerability into her big doelike eyes. She claimed it was the move, and granted, two thousand miles could put a little excitement into the most placid of people. Still, Mark had a feeling she was harboring more concerns than that.

Kim continued to say nothing, but as Mark drove home, he couldn't help noticing her interest in the passing scenery—covert turns of her head, lingering gazes down one avenue or another. Yet everytime she realized he was watching her, she'd cast her eyes down to her lap.

Mark felt a twinge of pity. Poor kid, she'd never traveled anywhere, and the chip on her shoulder was preventing her from enjoying even a simple drive.

"This isn't the way home." She sat up rigidly.

"Just a short detour." Mark circled a busy downtown block, then pulled to the side of a long broad avenue. "You've heard of Pike's Peak, I imagine."

She nodded guardedly. "'Pike's Peak or Bust.' That's what the pioneers used to write on their wagons when they headed West."

"Yes, during the gold-rush days of the 1880s." Mark pointed toward the blue-gray ridge capped with snow in the distance. "That's it." He watched her eyes widen, the irises deepening to bright onyx stars. "You can see the peak from almost anywhere in the city, but this street has the best view. It's called Pike's Peak Avenue, in fact."

Kim sat forward, her arms resting on the dash, her chin on her arms.

"Coming across the prairie, that was the first peak they saw. It's over 14,000 feet high," Mark explained, captivated by the faraway look in her eyes. "What are you thinking, Kim?" he asked gently.

"Oh...how difficult travel was back then, what a chance they took..." She sat back, tossing her head with indifference. "I wasn't thinking anything really."

Mark doubted that. He pulled back into the traffic. "During the summer, a cog railroad runs to the top. We'll go up sometime, okay? Would you like that?" Maybe if he gave her a sales pitch about the area, she'd be more inclined to sink roots. Miriam would appreciate that.

"You can tour old mines up there, places like Cripple Creek where people made unspeakable fortunes. And the view's incredible. It's what inspired the song 'America, the Beautiful.'" She still wasn't responding, and he sensed his patter was dwindling to nervous babble. He decided to shut up.

But he didn't head home just yet. He drove on, wondering what he could show her next. The Air Force Academy? The Olympic Training Center? The ancient Indian hot springs at Manitou? Should he show her anything at all? She was trying so hard to look bored, but dammit, he was beginning to get a kick out of introducing her to new things.

On an impulse, he drove by Brightman, Collins and Fuller. "That's where I work."

"Holy..." She swiveled in her seat as they passed the imposing Victorian mansion that had been converted to offices. Mark had all he could do not to laugh.

Before returning to the house, he took one more excursion, out to the 940-acre area called the Garden of the Gods. He felt compelled, not because the dramatic rock formations were so famous but because he had to see her face as they drove through. She didn't disappoint him.

Still, when they got home, she retired to her room with a sterile "Thanks for the tour" and sequestered herself with the typewriter for the rest of the afternoon.

Well, he'd tried. But if he hadn't reached her, so what? Did it really matter?

Mark prepared himself a frozen dinner, then called through Kim's door that there was an extra in the oven if she was hungry. After that he left for Suzanne's.

It was just as well Kim kept to herself, he thought again as he drove away. He didn't need another drain on his time. What he needed was an evening with Suzanne, a woman who was gracious, beautiful and far more his peer. Maybe then he'd be able to shake this feeling that his world was inexplicably turning upside down.

KIM SAT ON HER BED, legs folded like a pretzel, and let her exuberant pen flow across her journal. "The dirt is red here. Red! I couldn't believe it and so many times almost asked Mark to stop the car and let me out just to touch the darn stuff.

"We drove through the Garden of the Gods, huge red sandstone spires that made me feel I was on another planet. I think Mark was disappointed by my lack of reaction, but I simply couldn't speak for the lump in my throat.

"The city sprawls. So much space. Big, big blue sky. Air so clean and light it makes you dizzy. And the Rockies! They loom over the city like one of the great high mysteries of life, beckoning...

"I'm trying not to notice things, afraid I'll get too interested and start wanting to do things beyond my ability or means. I tell myself to shut things out, not look, not feel or smell or hear. But how?

"Already I'm feeling regret for experiences I'll probably never have. Like skiing, hiking, attending a rodeo. But those aren't my only regrets.

"Mark is as intriguing as this land I find myself in. In a perfect world, where age and education and class don't matter, I think we could be friends. Sometimes I think we could be more."

Kim stared at the sentence she'd just penned and felt her heart race. Wherever had that idea come from?

"I must find a job and get out of this house," she wrote quickly. "My mind, to say nothing of my resolve, disintegrates here."

WHEN MARK CAME downstairs the next morning, Kim was already washing the parlor walls. "Hi." She looked up from her pail to see him squinting against the sunlight. Dressed in navy sweats, hair disheveled, he looked anything but the high-powered lawyer he apparently was. "Rough night?"

He groaned.

Kim set to scrubbing extra hard, not caring to think about the cause of his fatigue.

"Do I smell coffee?" he mumbled.

"Uh-huh. And apple muffins just out of the oven."

Mark cocked his head. "Well, I'll be!" He set off down the hall. "Did Miriam teach you how to bake? She used to make a mean cherry cobbler when I was a kid."

"Uh, no. Miriam doesn't..." She paused. She couldn't remember the last time Miriam had cooked, but she didn't feel right messing with Mark's memories.

"What did you say?"

"Yes. She taught me everything I know." Kim rolled her eyes.

A few minutes later he rejoined her, looking far more alert. He set his coffee on a windowsill and pushed up his sleeves.

"What do you think you're doing?" she inquired.

"Move over." He dunked another sponge into the sudsy water.

By the end of the afternoon, they'd completed the parlor. Walls were washed, windows gleamed, woodwork glowed.

Sitting with her back against the wall, Kim watched tree shadows sway across the polished oak floor and smiled contentedly. "Looks great, doesn't it?"

She rolled her head to look at Mark, sitting on the floor beside her. He was admiring the fireplace that had taken him two full hours to clean. A smile lifted one corner of his mouth—his only response.

But then, they didn't have to say anything, she thought. Just as surely as they shared their tiredness, they shared a sense of satisfaction and joy in a job well done.

Odd. She didn't know many men who enjoyed their homes as much as Mark did. In fact, she didn't know any.

While they'd been working, she'd wanted to ask him dozens of questions, personal questions, but she'd also been aware that he didn't ask any of her. They'd listened to the radio and talked about their tasks. They'd kept to the moment, avoiding their pasts, avoiding their futures, their thoughts and their feelings—and she was glad. She wanted it that way, didn't she?

But now, sitting beside him, she felt they'd communicated, anyway. It had just happened.

The sound of a car stopping at the curb drew Kim's attention.

"Sounds like Suzanne," Mark said. "I wonder what—" He stopped and slapped his forehead. "I forgot. We're supposed to be reviewing a case she's working on." He blew out a long sigh. "Sorry about this, Kim."

The doorbell rang, and before either of them moved out of their indolent positions, Suzanne breezed into the foyer.

"Well, look at you two ragamuffins!" She smiled, as lovely as Kim remembered. Yet a chill seemed to descend on the room. Her eyes flicked from Mark to Kim, sitting so close their arms nearly touched "What've you been doing?"

Mark got to his feet and escorted Suzanne to the living room across the foyer, his explanation sounding painfully defensive. Left alone, Kim folded the ladder and carried it into the empty alcove, which she intended to tackle tomorrow. With that cleaned, she'd be able to move Mark's "office," and the day after that get started on the dining room.

"Kim?"

She jumped. "Yes, Mark?"

"Would you mind getting a couple of pizzas out of the freezer and throwing them into the microwave?"

Microwaved pizza? She pulled a face. "Sure."

Apparently Mark lived on frozen foods, she decided, surveying the contents of his freezer. She shook her head. They were okay in a pinch. But every day?

She opened a cupboard and stared at rows of canned vegetables. Small cans, the sort a lonely person buys, she thought unexpectedly.

Rubbish! Just because Mark lived alone didn't mean he was lonely. What it did mean was he had a lousy diet, and Ms. Brightman was too busy and high-powered herself to care.

Kim went back to the freezer and dug out a pound of hamburger. Lord only knew how old it was, but mixed into a shepherd's pie, she doubted Mark would notice. And, quite frankly, Kim didn't care if Suzanne did!

THE WEEK PASSED in a blur of activity. Starting on Monday, Kim shared the cleaning of the house with two other women, one from a temporary agency, the other Mark's cleaning woman, who, under normal circumstances, only came in once a week. Mark insisted on the extra help and Kim didn't object. There was certainly enough work to go around, and she did have other things to tend to.

Like filling in job applications and going for interviews. She also spent time driving, with no other purpose than to learn the city. She found the library, got a card and checked out two new child-care books. She found the supermarket, restocked the pantry, then reveled in a kitchen that was fitted out with every appliance ever invented. She ground fresh coffee beans and spit-roasted chicken, and one day she even made pasta.

Busy though she was, on Thursday she managed to wedge in a trip to the hairdresser. She'd phoned Suzanne to ask where she got her hair done, and the woman had replied quite readily—until she realized Kim meant to go there herself. Then she'd tried to backpedal by saying it was impossible to book an appointment unless one was a regular.

Afterward, Kim wished Suzanne had been more convincing. She almost cried, paying her bill. But when she looked at her reflection, she decided the hundred dollars was worth it. Finally someone had given her the cut and gentle perm she'd always dreamed of having. When Mark complimented her that evening, well, she decided she'd gotten a bargain.

It was a very good week, and when Miriam phoned on Friday to make sure Kim had reached Colorado in one piece, Kim was embarrassed by how many days had passed without her thinking of making this call herself. She assured Miriam she was settling in, then learned that nothing new had developed regarding the sale of the house.

"But the couple who put down the binder are now shopping for a mortgage. I can't guarantee it," Miriam hedged, "but I got a feeling this'll all be over in two, three weeks."

They hung up then because the movers from the rental center had arrived.

When Mark came home, everything was in its place. He set down his briefcase, loosened his tie and strode in slowly, his deep azure eyes taking it all in: the draperies that had taken Kim hours to iron, the Oriental rugs she'd argued for, the sparkle of the dining room chandelier. Waiting for his reaction, Kim realized her breath was caught in her throat.

This wasn't supposed to happen, she thought, chewing on her lip. They were supposed to have stayed uninvolved. Yet somehow his response had come to matter to her.

"This is great." He finally said, a lazy smile working across his sun-bronzed face.

"Do you really like it?"

"Are you kidding! Come here," he laughed.

She went to him before realizing what was coming. The next moment, he'd pulled her into his arms and was rocking her in a big affectionate hug.

"Thank you, kitten. You've been such a help."

Kitten? Kim stiffened and closed her eyes tight, trying to shut out the sight of him, the feel of him, the scent of him. But the sensations came through nonetheless. She was trembling when he finally let her go.

"Kim, are you all right?"

"Uh…yes. Just one last touch of Rocky Mountain high." As she spun away, she caught her reflection in the French doors that divided the parlor from the dining room. Lumpy sweats. Hair caught up with an untidy cord. Her heart sank.

She was being a first-class jerk, worrying about a friendly hug. Suzanne was the only type of woman Mark could possibly become interested in, and Suzanne probably didn't even own a pair of sweats, let alone a pair with a hole in one knee. Kim doubted he ever called her "kitten," either. Kitten. A helpless baby animal. An endearment for a child.

"You must be exhausted," Mark said. "How about if we go out to eat tonight?"

"Thanks, but I put a roast in the oven this afternoon. Should be almost done."

"You're spoiling me, Kimberly." He removed his suit jacket and hooked it over the stair newel.

"Well, don't get used to it." She tossed her head in mock indifference. "Come Monday, I'll be a working girl and won't be able to cook much anymore."

"You found a job? Already?"

"Two jobs. Calls started coming in yesterday. I picked what I thought were the best offers."

"Well, I'll be." He looked astounded.

"I accepted a full-time waitressing job, evenings. And four afternoons a week, I'll be doing light office work at a downtown department store."

Mark walked to the bar and poured himself a splash of Irish Mist. He stared at the glass for a while without saying anything, a meditative frown crossing his face. "Congratulations," he finally said, tossing back the drink.

SATURDAY MORNING, Kim tipped the sugar bowl, spilling sugar over the kitchen table. She couldn't believe how nervous she was, and she wasn't even going to attend Mark's party. She'd walk around a mall, sit in a movie theater, do anything to avoid it.

"Kim, the florist will be here soon," Mark said, helping her scoop up the mess, "but I have to run by the office for a while." He raised his eyebrows in an unspoken question. She nodded an unspoken of course, she'd accept the delivery.

"You're a peach. This afternoon I want you to do something for yourself for a change." Mark pulled his checkbook from the inside pocket of his jacket. "I want you to go shopping for something to wear tonight."

Kim froze. He studied her stunned silence a moment.

"I don't know how else to repay you for all the help you've given me this week."

"But I thought . . . I wasn't planning to be here tonight."

Mark looked confused. "But you have to. I need you."

"You need me?" Kim laughed. "This party's as organized as the landing at Normandy."

"But I can't be everywhere. I'll be busy with my guests. What if something goes wrong in the kitchen?"

During the week, their policy of noninvolvement had grown thoroughly murky, and again she wondered how. She'd tried to keep her affairs to herself, and Mark had been busy with work. Yet, somehow a vine of caring had twined through their relationship.

"Okay, I'll be here." She sipped her coffee nervously. "But I don't need a new dress."

"Please," he insisted. In gratitude? She doubted it. More likely, he was still afraid her appearance would embarrass him.

He opened the checkbook and filled in everything but the amount. "Here." He leaned across the table and pressed the check into her hand. "Get yourself a nice dress. Something understated, demure. You look good in pink."

"And should I wear my hair in braids?" she asked with contrived sauciness. She felt bad immediately. Her living here was obviously a sticky situation for Mark. "How are you going to introduce me? As your niece?"

"May I?"

"I guess." Kim didn't much care for the deceit, slight though it was, but apparently the senior partners were rather elderly and straitlaced. Appearances were important to them.

Of course she had no intention of using Mark's check. She already had a dress she could wear, even if it was a little outdated. But who was going to pay attention to her anyway, especially if she kept to the kitchen?

She did go shopping, though, because she needed new stockings. On a whim, she bought them in one of the expensive shops Mark had recommended. Having made the purchase, she was reluctant to leave. The new spring line was in, and as she browsed, Kim played a game of imagining she could afford anything she wanted. She'd played the game often enough back home at Macy's and Bloomingdale's, but never with a blank check in her purse. Somehow that lent the game a reality that was almost palpable.

She still couldn't believe he'd handed it to her. Just like that. Didn't he know what she could do with a blank check? She could get on a plane and fly to New York ... fly to Tahiti if she dared. She could go to a bank, wipe out his account, and run....

She took the check from her purse and studied his signature, each bold dash and curve. She'd never known such unmitigated trust. Maybe it deserved something in return.

THE HOUSE WAS WARM and crowded and throbbed with conversations that all but drowned out the music coming from the four stereo speakers. Mark's gaze swept the gathering as he continued to talk to Milton Barnes, the owner of a local construction company. The party was off to a good start.

Mark didn't like Milton Barnes. He never had. Before coming to Brightman, Collins and Fuller, he'd represented a couple who'd bought a house in one of Barnes's developments, a house that fell far short of what they'd expected. Mark had won a settlement in their favor, but not nearly what they'd deserved. A master at cutting corners while still remaining within the law, Barnes had been too slippery. Even now Mark saw red when he remembered that suit.

Now Brightman, Collins and Fuller wanted to take Barnes on as a client. They wanted to reel him in, and it was up to Mark to do the reeling. That was tonight's mission.

Mark was nodding through an enervating discussion about a new computer system Milton had recently purchased when he finally spotted the crown of Kim's curly auburn hair over the crowd. He hadn't seen her since she'd gone up to dress, and he was beginning to fear she'd decided not to come down.

He was glad she had. He'd missed her. During the past week he'd grown used to her company. He'd never lived with anyone before and was just beginning to realize what a void Kim filled. It would be nice having her—and Miriam—living close by.

The crowd between them parted, and suddenly Kim came into full view. Mark's heart stopped.

"Oh, mercy!" His softly muttered words were out before he knew it.

Barnes turned, following Mark's gaze. "Well! Who's this?"

Mark watched Kim approach, her brown eyes wide and doelike. He told himself she was just a scared little girl inside, but Lord, on the outside tonight she was all woman.

She was wearing a short sleeveless black dress that clung to curves he hadn't even known she had, sheer black stockings and high-heeled shoes, thinly strapped around the ankles, that made her shapely legs seem to go on forever. And that hair, that glorious mane of auburn curls—she'd done something to it that made it look slightly wild and definitely sexy.

"Good evening, Kimberly," he somehow got out.

"Mark." She was wearing makeup tonight, applied so artfully her features looked ethereal. Yet, despite her confident appearance, Mark saw that her smile was shy.

Barnes cleared his throat, obviously waiting for an introduction.

"Milton, this is my sister's daughter, Kimberly Wade. Kim, Mr. Barnes."

Barnes took Kim's hand and lowered his lips to it. "Please, call me Milton."

Kim's long eyelashes fluttered in surprise. "How do you do?"

He smiled charmingly, while Mark did a slow burn. Barnes was at least twenty years older than Kim, but he was in top physical shape, and most women, Mark heard, con-

sidered him quite handsome. He was witty, urbane—and a
top-notch sleaze. Everybody knew he'd made scoring a second career, and right now Kim looked to be his next target.
He'd already taken her arm and was gliding away with her.

Mark stepped in their path. "Excuse us a minute. I
promised my sister Kim would call home at—" he glanced
at his watch "—right about now. She'll be back soon."

Mark gripped Kim's arm, all too aware of its warm silky
softness, and propelled her toward the kitchen. There, ignoring the looks of the kitchen help, he corralled her against
a counter. Her perfume made his head light.

"What's wrong?" she asked, her lips parted. "Have I
done something already?"

He stared at her mouth, at those full ripe lips. "No. I..."
What was he doing? Why was he reacting so strongly?
Barnes had only said hello. "Nothing. I just wanted to tell
you that you look nice." Nice? *Nice?* Kim lit the house like
a fireworks display.

"Thanks." She looked at him suspiciously.

"And be careful, kitten. Barnes is a shark."

As soon as they returned, Mark noticed that one of the
other attorneys at Brightman, Collins and Fuller had latched
onto Barnes. Stu Zambroski. Mark shook his head, half
pitying, half amused.

He'd made enemies in his day, proudly so, but only one
whose animosity sprang solely from ambition. Stu Zambroski had been hired the same year as Mark and from the
very beginning had measured their careers, inch by slow
inch. The gossip flying about Mark's impending promotion obviously did not sit well with him. Right now, Stu was
probably hoping to undercut whatever progress he believed
Mark had made with Barnes.

If only Zambroski knew how relieved Mark was to be free
of Barnes for a while. He'd resented having to invite him
into his home, resented the position the partners had put

him in. Stu could have Barnes with Mark's blessing. Now at least he had a moment to spend with Kim.

Just then, however, a pair of cool arms encircled his neck. "Mark, love!" Suzanne kissed him fully on the mouth. "You're a genius! This place looks wonderful!"

"Hi, Suzanne." He backed off, his eyes fixed on Kim as she threaded her way through the parlor. She had a glass of champagne in one hand and was smiling up at a tall young man. Who *was* that? Mark wondered irritably. Ah, yes. Bill Fuller's son. First year law school. Smart, good-looking, bright future.

"Is that Kim?" Suzanne's eyes widened. "My Lord!"

"Can I get you a drink, Sue?"

"No, thanks. Will you look at that dress!" With a smile that wasn't at all kind, she drifted into the parlor. Mark tensed with protectiveness and set out after her, but Suzanne merely said a polite hello and continued on her way.

Mark's shoulders sagged. What was happening to his good sense? Suzanne had no reason to act catty. Kim was his niece. Well, stepniece. He had to pull himself together, get Kim out of his mind. He had forty other guests to tend to.

"So, what's Kim doing here?" Milton Barnes had apparently shaken Zambroski, who was glowering across the room, and purposely sought Mark out. "Is she on vacation?"

Mark was tempted to say yes and that she was leaving the next day. "No. She and my sister are moving here from the East Coast. My sister's still there, selling their house."

"She's quite a beauty."

Mark was quickly figuring that out. "She's also very young."

Barnes grinned into his fluted glass. "All the better."

Mark's jaw clenched. "I'm serious."

"Really?" Barnes's stare became a challenge. "You wouldn't be trying to keep her all to yourself, would you?"

"Don't be stupid. She's my niece. I feel responsible." Mark was sure steam was shooting from his ears, but this was neither the time nor the place for confrontation. "Just... leave her alone, okay?" He noticed two of the partners watching him and attempted a smile before striding off, but he was sure his contempt for Barnes ruined the effect.

Mark milled among his guests, pleased they were having a good time. The food was superb, his house comfortable, and a small group had loosened up enough to turn the sun porch into a dance floor. Even old man Collins was out there, moving his stiff unexercised bulk in something that looked suspiciously like the twist.

Kim seemed to be a success, too. Especially with Milton Barnes. In spite of Mark's warning, he had her trapped at one end of the sofa for the better part of an hour, thinking, no doubt, he was charming her with his sparkling wit. For most of the hour Mark told himself to back off. They were only talking. But when Kim finally got up, excusing herself to go to the powder room, she shot Mark a look of agony.

"Say, Johnson, I've got a deal for you," Barnes said.

Mark wanted to throttle the creep. Instead, he pulled in a deep calming breath. Barnes was, after all, a guest in his house, and the partners *were* expecting Mark to court him tonight. "What can I do for you?"

"Fix it so she goes out with me."

"Who? Kim?"

"Mmm. I'm not sure I'm getting anywhere with her. How about applying a little pressure on the home front, eh?" He cuffed Mark's arm and grinned.

Mark returned a withering stare. "A deal, huh? And what do I get in return?"

Barnes's grin broadened. "You're a smart guy. You figure it out." He strode off, leaving Mark gripping his drink so hard he feared the glass would shatter.

When Kim returned, Mark was relieved to see Fuller's son commandeer her to the sun porch for a dance. He was a nice young man, clean-cut, well-mannered, the exact sort a father would like to see his daughter date. *That* was why he was relieved, Mark told himself, not because the boy was on spring break and would be returning to college in a few days.

Satisfied Kim was safe, Mark allowed Suzanne to monopolize him for a time. Over her smooth blond head, he noticed that Zambroski had buttonholed Barnes again and was talking up a storm. Mark's mouth tightened. Stu's jealousy and paranoia were no longer amusing.

Suzanne tugged him across the room to meet a prominent local politician, who pumped his hand and launched into what was sure to be a future campaign speech. When Mark finally managed to get away, he searched the room, but Milton Barnes had disappeared. Mark strode to the sun porch and saw Barnes pulling Kim into his arms while a red-faced young man stepped aside.

"Careful, love," Suzanne said. "You'll end up in a stroke ward before the night is over."

Mark tried to laugh. "Well, you know Barnes's reputation. And Kim *is* my responsibility."

"She's a big girl. She can take care of herself."

Mark downed his drink in one swig. She *was* a big girl. That was what bothered him. She had every right to go out with whomever she pleased, and he had no right to interfere.

He rocked on his leather-soled shoes, hands jammed into his pants pockets, and watched them dance. Kim, so young, fresh, vulnerable—being charmed by that silver-tongued sleaze.

Mark rocked a bit longer, reminding himself that the deal was nearly in the bag. Without any complicated negotiations, Barnes had implied he'd hire the firm as his legal counsel. All Mark had to do was stand back, look away.

He tried. He looked at Suzanne. He looked at other women he'd taken out, to women he could take out in the future if he wished. The house was full of them. But the silent pressure rising inside him finally blew its gauge, and before he realized what he was doing, he'd crossed the room.

The tap on Barnes's shoulder was more a shove. "Pardon me, but I believe the lady would like to take a break."

Barnes kept his arms locked around Kim's waist. "You're beginning to get on my nerves, Johnson."

"I'm going to get on more than that if you don't let her go." Mark noticed relief in Kim's eyes.

"If you don't mind," she said kindly, "I *would* like to spend more time mingling. I was looking forward to meeting new people tonight."

"Of course." Barnes bowed graciously, but as soon as she was gone, he shot Mark a venomous glare. "You don't seem to understand the terms of the deal, Johnson."

Mark was aware that a lot was on the line. A fourteen-million-dollar business. A coup in the eyes of his employers. And quite possibly the career step he'd been working toward for nearly ten years.

And suddenly none of it amounted to a tinker's damn.

CHAPTER FIVE

KIM WAS BUSILY WRITING down the caterer's recipe for spinach quiche when Mark walked into the kitchen. She glanced up. "Hi. Everybody gone?"

He nodded. "Is this where you've been hiding?"

Hiding? Yes, she supposed that was exactly what she'd been doing.

Mark leaned his hip against the counter. "Sorry about Barnes."

"Thanks for the rescue." She really meant it. No one had ever stood up for her the way Mark had. She was used to fending for herself and could have done so again tonight. Still, Mark's chivalry had touched her.

Mark glanced at the caterer and her two helpers. "You people must be bushed. How about coming by in the morning to clean up, hmm?"

When they were finally alone, he took Kim into the parlor. "What a disaster."

"I'm glad we rented."

"Me, too."

"Oh, here, I meant to give you this earlier." She pulled his check from her pocket.

Mark took it and frowned. "Didn't you go shopping?"

"Yes. But I used my own money."

"Kim, that dress must've cost you a fortune."

"Hardly. It was winter stock. I got it on sale, seventy-five percent off." Still, the money she'd come here with was now almost depleted. She'd be starting work none too soon.

Mark's gaze traveled from her head to her high-heeled shoes. "Well, you look like a million."

Heat bloomed in Kim's cheeks. "So? How did it go?" She settled herself onto a footstool by the fireplace.

"The party?" Mark stretched out on the couch.

"No. How did *you* do?"

"What do you mean?"

"Well, I know what you said about this party having nothing to do with your promotion, but I'm not blind, Mark. The partners were watching you all night. So, did you prove to them what a good team player you are?"

He chuckled. "Ah, me! Afraid not."

Kim's back straightened. "Why not?"

Mark looked at her, his steady stare burning into her. His face, made handsomer still by the dim lamplight, grew serious. "They weren't pleased by the way I handled Milton Barnes. You see, he fired the lawyers who used to represent him and is shopping around for a new firm."

"Milton Barnes?" Kim winced. "Oh, Mark, I'm sorry."

"Shh. I've never liked him. Telling him off felt good."

"You didn't!"

Mark tucked a pillow under his head. "Afraid so, kitten." He seemed to be fond of calling her kitten.

"Who was that other creep, the one with the receding hairline?"

"Zambroski? He works for the firm, too. Did you meet him?"

"No, but I didn't have to to know he isn't exactly your best friend. I have a sixth sense about some people." Kim watched Mark watching her, his eyes glittering a deep violet blue. He had such a direct honest stare, reaching deep inside her.

"What else did that sixth sense pick up tonight?"

"Well, half the women here tonight have either dated you or are hoping to. I tell you, Mark, it makes me wonder what sort of Casanova Miriam entrusted me to." This made Mark laugh heartily. "Well, am I right?"

Still chuckling, Mark made a so-so motion with his hand. "I've dated some."

"Yeah, sure. You were just looking for the right woman and couldn't find her, right?"

"Something like that."

"What about Suzanne?"

"What about her?"

Kim shifted uneasily when she recalled how Suzanne had been hanging on Mark's arm every time she'd looked over. "Is she going to be the one?"

"And what makes you think I want to settle down?"

Kim shrugged self-consciously. "Just a notion. This big homey house. The fact that you coach at the Boys Club because you don't have kids of your own and wish you did."

Mark grabbed a pillow and flung it at her head. "Knock it off."

Grinning smugly, Kim picked up the pillow and smoothed it across her knees. "Pegged you, didn't I?"

"Let's change the subject. What did you think of Curly, Larry and Moe?"

"Who?"

"The esteemed partners."

"Oh." Kim giggled. "They terrified me. Such austere serious men, all three of them. I actually choked on an olive when you introduced me to the tall one."

Mark smiled. "You covered yourself well."

A frown tightened her brow. "They don't like me much, especially Suzanne's father. I heard him and Mr. Collins passing remarks about how my living here doesn't look right. I guess I should've taken your advice and bought something pink and demure."

"Don't let them throw you. They're flawed just like the rest of us." His gaze was warm, nearly a caress. "Know something? This is nice, sitting here, having someone to talk to late at night.''

Yes, Kim thought. Almost like being married.

"Hey, are you hungry?"

"Famished,'' she said eagerly. "I was too nervous to eat. We have lots of leftovers.''

"Sounds good.'' Mark started to get up.

"No, I'll get it. You stay.''

He smiled contentedly, more contentedly, Kim thought, than a man should after spending an evening cutting his own throat.

When she returned from the kitchen, Mark was asleep. She smiled, watching him snore lightly.

Kitten. She tried to feel like the little pet he had in mind. But as she watched his broad chest softly rise and fall, as she followed the lines of his long indolent body and studied the sensuous curve of his mouth, she didn't feel like that sort of kitten. Not that sort at all.

KIM STARTED WORK at the Blue Lantern restaurant the next week, and although it was only a Monday night, tips were phenomenal. Having worked as long as she had, her instincts were honed sharp, and she'd known this would be a gold mine. The place catered to a steak-lobster-and-bourbon crowd, a crowd that lingered deep into the night because there was entertainment.

You couldn't have everything, though, she admitted, as she shimmied out of her "uniform" and back into street clothes at the end of the night, which was actually 2 a.m. The outfit she'd had to wear was supposedly a peasant dress, to go along with the restaurant's vaguely European-country decor. It had a puff-sleeved off-the-shoulder top and a string-cinched waist, which looked "country" enough, she supposed, but the gathered skirt barely covered her behind.

Still, she couldn't complain. The money was good and added to what she made at her afternoon job, she figured she'd have saved a couple of thousand dollars by the time Miriam arrived.

Kim felt a familiar hot pull of tension as she thought about Miriam. And Theodore. And the possibility that he might follow Miriam out here. If he did, if Miriam married him... Kim hated to dwell on her dark insecurities, but they were there nonetheless, prodding her to work and to save.

As the week progressed, she realized she and Mark had very little chance to see each other and even less to talk. She came in late, slept all morning, and by the time he returned from the office, she was already gone again. During the few rare minutes when their paths did cross, Kim couldn't help noticing he looked tired and agitated.

"You okay?" she asked on Thursday. That was the one afternoon she didn't go into the office. Mark had come home purposely to share an early supper with her.

"Yes, fine." He smiled forcibly, but lines remained etched between his brows. Something was apparently wrong. At work? she wondered. The botched deal with Milton Barnes?

She tried to convince herself that wasn't her concern. She should be thankful their schedules were causing them to drift apart. Instead, she ached with a desire to put her arms around him in a big comforting hug.

"How's work?" he asked.

"Great." But she knew she was frowning, too. She was making good money at the Lantern, so it shouldn't matter that her sixth sense was picking up disturbing vibes about the place.

"Well, you look tired. Take it easy."

"Can't afford to."

Mark's scowl deepened. "Milton Barnes has been asking about you."

Kim put down her fork. "You haven't told him anything, have you?"

"No." He paused, measuring her expression. "The guy's worth about fourteen million, you know.'

"Good for him." She shoveled another forkful of potato salad into her mouth. Mark smiled and her heart warmed. "I'm sorry your firm lost his business, though."

Mark pushed his food around his plate. "We didn't lose him. He signed on yesterday. Zambroski got him." Mark stood up, scraped the remains of his meal into the disposal and put the plate in the dishwasher.

Kim's heart plummeted. "Is this going to affect your promotion?"

"No, of course not. If it does, I work for fools." He caught her eye. "Really. Don't worry about it."

Dubious though she was, she changed the subject. "When's the rented furniture leaving?"

"It's not. I extended the lease indefinitely, at least until I can buy furniture of my own. It's nice being able to use all the rooms."

"Mmm." Kim put her plate in the dishwasher, too, and wiped off the table. "Have you talked to Miriam this week?"

"No. You?"

"Uh-uh. I wonder how she's doing with the house."

"Maybe I'll give her a call tonight."

"Good. Could you tell her I've been too busy to go looking at apartments, but I will soon?"

"Sure." Mark fell silent, staring out the sink window. Kim hoped he was right and she hadn't jeopardized his chances of advancement at the firm, but she probably had. She was the reason Mark and Milton Barnes had locked horns.

All the more reason for her to focus on her own life. The faster she got out of his, the sooner it would mend.

"Got to go," she said, slipping on her coat.

He turned abruptly. "Already?"

"Uh-huh. See you... whenever." She hoped she didn't sound as downhearted as she felt.

MARK STOOD at the kitchen door long after Kim had driven off, taking in the soft March evening. He wasn't sure he liked her working so many hours. He didn't know why she was doing it. Though they'd relaxed around each other somewhat, she still kept so much of herself concealed. Surely her father's death had left her financially free of the necessity to work, at least for a while.

But even more exasperating than not knowing why she was working was the fact that it completely blew his initial image of her. No direction? No drive? Good Lord, the girl was practically obsessed with ambition!

He rubbed his eyes and turned from the door. The house was awfully quiet. Too quiet. Mark wandered down the hall through the parlor into his new study. There he picked up the phone and punched in Miriam's number.

He leaned against his desk as the call went through and someone answered at the other end. But it wasn't his sister. It was a fuzzy recording telling him the number he'd dialed had been disconnected.

Mark hung up in a thoughtful daze. Disconnected? Why would Miriam disconnect her phone without telling them? How were they to get in touch if an emergency arose? Was it possible she'd sold the house and already moved out?

Mark jammed his hands into the pockets of his trousers and paced across the book-lined room. Where the hell was Miriam *now?* He laughed mirthlessly. It seemed he'd been asking that question all his life.

Mark paused at his desk where Kim had tossed one of her sweaters, a huge blue thing that smelled of potato chips and something floral, like her hair. Mark smiled. Her hair. That gorgeous mane of auburn curls he hated to see bound up when she went off to work. Hair like that should always be left free to fly.

He stroked the soft knit and remembered the feel of her skin. He'd been trying to stay out of her way, to not think about her or the secrets in her eyes, but the truth was, he could think of little else these days.

He yanked the phone off the desk again and called New York information. But, no, there was no other number listed under the name of Miriam Wade, or Johnson, or any of her other names acquired over the course of her marriages.

Mark paced the room a few minutes more before returning to the desk and flipping the Rolodex.

"Hi, Bob? Mark Johnson here."

The voice at the other end swore in good-natured surprise. "How have you been, my friend?"

"Good. Good. I hope I'm not interrupting anything, Bob, but I've got a little problem." Mark and Bob Cooper had gone to college together and had remained friends in spite of the distance that separated them. Bob, a law school dropout, had set himself up as a private investigator and ran a thriving practice in New York.

When Mark hung up, he felt much better. If anybody could get to the bottom of this missing-sister mystery, it was Bob. Not that Mark really believed there was a mystery. Any day now, Miriam would call with an explanation, and before he knew it, she'd be here, filling his life with her smile and bright chatter.

Mark stretched out on his recliner. He opened a book, started to read and promptly went to sleep.

HE AWOKE WITH A START, his reading glasses tumbling off his nose and down his chest. Then the phone rang, apparently for the second time. He eased himself from the chair and picked up the receiver.

"Hmm." Sleepily, he glanced at his watch.

"Mark?"

He became alert instantly. "Kim?" Her voice sounded so small. "What's up, kitten? Something happen to the car?" It was after one in the morning, and the thought of her out there broken down did funny things to his stomach.

"Umm, no. Your car's fine."

"Are you still at work?"

"No." Her voice was getting smaller. Mark could hear movement in the background—voices, footsteps, phones ringing.

"I'm sorry to disturb you, but I didn't know what else to do. They've allowed me this one call and—"

Alarm jolted through him. "Where are you?"

"At the police station."

He sank into his desk chair. "Good Lord! Have you been arrested?"

"Sorta."

Mark reined in a surge of confused emotions. "What does 'sorta' mean?"

"Well, the restaurant was raided tonight and we all got pulled in—waitresses, busboys, everybody."

"What exactly is the name of this restaurant, Kimberly?"

"You're mad, aren't you? You're calling me Kimberly."

"The name." Why hadn't he paid closer attention?

"The Blue Lantern."

"Blue Lantern," he repeated, letting the name fall through the tumblers of his mind. "Terrific," he spat as the reference clicked.

"I think it's a front for something, but honestly, Mark, I had no idea."

"All right, enough." His voice was sharper than intended. "I'll be there in a few minutes. What station?"

She told him and he hung up, too agitated even to say goodbye.

"KIM WADE?" A policewoman stood in the doorway of the holding room. "Your ride's here."

Kim shot to her feet.

"Good luck, honey," said the cocktail waitress who was also waiting to be released. "Hope you find another job real soon."

"What? Oh, yes. You too." The last concern on Kim's mind at the moment was getting another job. What bothered her now was facing Mark. She burned with humiliation just thinking about it. How could she have been so stupid, going to work at a place that was a front for illegal gambling?

Even worse than her poor judgment, however, was this uniform. As Kim walked down the corridor toward the front desk, she tried to tug up the bodice, but that only hiked up the skirt. How would Mark ever respect her after this?

Respect? That was a laugh. She'd be lucky if Mark didn't already have her bags packed. Counting the complication with Milton Barnes, this was the second serious mess she'd caused in a week, and her old conviction, that she never should have left New York, returned.

Mark was talking to the officer at the desk. Kim got the feeling it wasn't the first time they'd met. Wonderful, she thought. She was embarrassing him in front of people he knew.

The officer noticed her and nodded in her direction. Kim slouched, hoping again to cover her thighs.

Mark turned slowly, as if bracing himself. Still, when he saw her, he did a slight double take. His reaction was almost imperceptible, yet in that heartbeat of time, she knew he'd taken in the whole package—the "peasant" dress, the red high-heeled shoes, the extra makeup the manager had suggested she wear. Kim wanted to slink through the floor tiles.

"Ready, Kim?" Mark asked calmly.

Her throat was so tight she could only nod.

"Where's your coat?"

She tried to say it was back at the restaurant but, again unable to speak, she only shrugged.

Mark slanted a steely glance at the officer. "This how you treat your prisoners these days, Newcombe?" The young man's ears turned pink as Mark slipped off his jacket and draped it over Kim's shoulders. It reached to her knees.

"Thank you," she somehow got out.

Just then, her attention shifted to a commotion rising from the corridor across the way. In the middle of the jostling was the man who owned the Blue Lantern. The scene looked like something from the six o'clock news—a few reporters, police, a lawyer or two, everyone shouting and circling this one snarling figure. Then it hit her; this probably *would* be on the six o'clock news.

"Come on. Let's get out of here." Mark gripped her elbow and hauled her across the lobby.

"Just like that? I don't have to sign any papers or post bail?"

"Of course not. It was a raid. You were only a guppy pulled up in the net."

"Hey, counselor, what you doing here?" came a curious insinuative voice.

Before Kim could even lift her eyes—or close Mark's jacket—a flash went off in her face.

She felt Mark's ire rise like a hot tide, quivering through his muscles. Yet she was amazed to hear him chuckle. "Get out of my face, Lenox," he said jovially.

Lenox, who was obviously a newspaper reporter, winked at the photographer with him, and another flash went off. Then he flipped open his spiral notepad with one hand and fell into step beside them. "What's happened to you, Johnson? How come you're playing in the streets with us common folk tonight?" His eyes moved from Mark to Kim, curiosity lending them a sharpness that unsettled her.

"Your story's getting away," Mark commented dryly with a nod back toward the lobby.

"What story? Lou Beecham gets pulled in for racketeering again?" He pulled a face of pure boredom. "Now, if I could get a few interesting quotes from somebody on the inside..." His eyes fixed on Kim again.

Her trembling was visible now, and the dizziness she thought she'd overcome was back.

Mark stopped in his tracks and squared off against the reporter. "There's no story here, Lenox, so take your..." He paused to pull in a breath. When he continued, he sounded calmer. "She isn't one of Beecham's runners. She'd just an innocent kid who's been employed at the Lantern all of four days."

"Oh, yeah? So, why are you here, counselor? Is it possible she's the daughter of somebody we both might know and love?" Lenox was still angling, probably hoping she was the wayward offspring of some local politician. His persistence made Kim shudder, with fear, but more with anger. Mark didn't need this hassle. He'd been up at seven every morning this week and had worked well into each night. She knew. She'd found him asleep in his recliner whenever she'd come in from work.

"For pity's sake!" She stepped from behind Mark's back, planting her hands on her hips. "I'm nobody important. I'm his stepniece, Kim Wade. That's all."

She couldn't tell if the reporter was disappointed or even more intrigued. All she knew was that Mark tensed.

"W-a-d-e-?" Lenox spelled out.

"Yes."

"Why on earth did you choose a place like the Blue Lantern, Miss Wade? Didn't your uncle warn you?"

"Always good seeing you, Lenox." Mark took Kim's arm and propelled her toward his waiting car, his shoes striking the pavement hard and fast.

"I'm sorry." She didn't know what else to say as they zoomed away from the curb. "I'm sorry," she repeated, pressing her hand against her right eye where a tear threatened to form.

He said nothing, and it didn't take a genius to figure out he was angry. In silence he threaded his way through the grid of long city boulevards, up, down, across. Kim huddled into his jacket, glad of its warmth, but more appreciative of the kindness and understanding that had put it there.

She turned her face aside. Best not to start thinking of Mark as some knight in shining armor. Most likely, he'd only wanted to protect his own image.

"Where are we going?"

"Just driving. Driving helps me work out the demons."

"Eating chocolate helps me." She hoped that was a smile tugging at his mouth.

"Your Cherokee's still back at the Lantern."

"Don't worry about the Cherokee. The police'll return it. I gave my key to a friend at the station."

"My clothes are still there, too."

"Forget the clothes. We'll buy others." He appeared almost eager.

Kim averted her face to hide her pain. How much of an embarrassment was she to him, anyway?

She watched the night drift by. The streets seemed to be rising away from the city into the foothills. When she looked back minutes later, the view stole her breath. All the twinkling lights of Colorado Springs were spread out below, and beyond stretched the great dark prairie.

They reached a turnaround at the end of a quiet road. Mark flicked off the engine but remained staring out over the city, his eyes intent, his jaw hard. He drew a deep breath, and Kim braced herself, expecting him to launch into a tirade about her job, about her uniform, about her risking his reputation. She waited, mentally framing her defense, coiled tight with tension...

"How are you doing?" he asked, instead. His voice was surprisingly soft.

"Okay, I guess." She pressed her hands against her cheeks to still their sudden quivering.

He reached over and rubbed her tight aching shoulders, his comforting touch the last thing she expected. "It must've been frightening."

Damn him. Why was sympathy so much harder to handle than anger? Anger would've toughened her. It was what she knew. But this, this was uncharted territory, and she was afraid she was getting lost fast.

"Kind of," she admitted. "I've never been arrested before."

"Well, it's all over. Relax, kitten."

That did it. Wrung out both physically and emotionally, Kim let go of her toughness and with a wobbly voice admitted, "Oh, Mark, it was awful."

"I know. Come here." He lifted his arms and she leaned toward him, letting him tuck her into his warm embrace. For a long while he held her against him, stroking her hair. She could feel his heart beating its strong reassuring rhythm, could feel his solidity and strength, and a sense of security she'd rarely known enveloped her. After a while the tightness in her throat eased, and a languorous peace washed through her. She wished she didn't have to move, ever.

Unfortunately the console between them was jabbing her ribs, and without his jacket, Mark was undoubtedly getting cold. She eased herself back to her seat.

"You must be freezing."

He smiled, a half grin that reached into her so deep she became momentarily confused. "Only this arm." He hitched his left shoulder. "It's the only part you weren't covering. But that's okay. It's so numb right now I don't even know I've got a problem."

"Is that supposed to make me feel better?" Kim started to remove his jacket, but he tugged it back on her.

"I'm fine, honest." He flicked on the ignition, and a shaft of disappointment shot through her.

"Do we have to go already?"

"No. Just turning on the heater."

"Oh, good." She wanted to remain, alone with him, wrapped in this cocoon of caring forever. "It's too beautiful up here," she said quickly, using the scenery as an excuse. "All those lights, with nothing beyond but dark empty plains stretching forever and that huge bright sky overhead . . ."

Mark's smile broadened. "Kim, I swear you're more taken with our plains than you are with—"

"With the mountains? Not really. The mountains just aren't real for me yet. They're so immense and overpowering, I guess I won't allow them to be real. One world wonder at a time, please."

Small fan lines feathered out from Mark's eyes as he studied her. Returning his smile, Kim was amazed that any man could possess so much appeal. It took effort to keep her mind on their conversation.

"Doesn't all this immenseness ever make you feel small?" she asked.

"Humble. That's the word I'd choose, Kim. You shouldn't ever let anything make you feel small."

Kim clutched her hands in her lap. All her life, people and circumstances seemed to have inspired to make her feel just that.

"Mark? Why aren't you packing me off to the airport right now?"

He turned fully in his seat, leaning his back against the door. Starlight, brighter than she'd ever seen anywhere, silvered his features. "What are you talking about?"

"Well, why are you being so understanding about this Blue Lantern thing?"

Mark was quiet for nearly a full minute, his eyes fixed on her but unfocused. Kim sensed he'd left the here and now and had drifted somewhere far and past. "I've worked in some pretty questionable places myself, Kim," he finally confessed. "My father died when I was nine. Life wasn't always easy."

Kim opened her mouth but nothing came out. Mark was a lawyer. He lived in a large gracious house and had influential friends. He employed a cleaning woman, drove a BMW. She assumed he'd always lived this way.

"Where are you from, Mark?" she asked, surprised she didn't know. Miriam had never shared much of her past.

"A little town out there." He pointed into the dark starsprinkled nothingness.

Kim blinked. "There are towns our there?"

"Uh-huh. About seventy miles that way we had a farm." His laugh was brittle. "Yeah, I guess it was a farm, though after my father died, it was pretty hard to tell."

"What sort of farm? Cows? Chickens? Geese?"

"Mostly it was alfalfa, acres and acres of boring alfalfa. Miriam and I, sometimes we used to sit up late at night talking about what we planned to do when we grew up. Of course, all those dreams began with getting away from the farm." His voice softened to a husky wistfulness. "Most nights, Miriam's plan was to hitch out to Hollywood and become an actress. That, or stow away on a freighter to Spain where she'd marry a wealthy count."

"And what were your dreams, Mark?" Kim whispered.

"Mine? Well, they usually involved riding the nose of a rocket to Mars. That or riding wild broncs in a rodeo."

Quiet as the night, Kim sat back, listening to Mark reminisce. Something was making her decidedly wary.

"But the details, Kim, the details Miriam added, they're what really made those nights special." He smiled, and Kim pinpointed the source of her unease. It was his affection for Miriam. "That sister of mine could go on for ten minutes just describing shrimp cocktail, which she assured me we'd eat all the time when we were rich. I didn't even know what it was, but I sure as hell could taste it. Lying out in the backyard on a hot summer night, she'd tell me all about the Cadillac Coupe de Villes we'd drive, too. Pink for her, blue for me. And the black Stetson hat I'd wear with a genuine silver-and-turquoise band...."

Mark paused, lowered his head and shrugged. "Ah, well..." That's all he said, but Kim understood his sense of loss.

"When did she leave?"

"The winter I was ten. She was seventeen and ready for the bright lights of Denver. A few months later we heard she was married." The silence that followed lengthened. Mark's smile faded until all the lines of his face were sad.

"And what did you do?"

"Me? I helped my mother as much as I could, but I had school. I could only do so much." He looked away, his profile hard. "She lost the place on the auction block the summer after I graduated high school." He shook his head slightly, the only indication of the anger and frustration Kim was sure he felt.

"After the auction, we packed up and went to Denver, too, but by then Miriam had already moved on."

Kim glanced up. Odd, she thought. Had they gone to Denver hoping to meet up with Miriam? Hadn't she bothered to keep in touch? But Kim didn't ask. She sensed that Mark preferred to remember Miriam as a girl spinning dreams on soft summer nights rather than the hard self-centered adult she'd become. Maybe he wasn't even aware of the change, and suddenly Kim realized the last thing she wanted to do was enlighten him.

"Is your mother still in Denver?"

Mark shook his head. "She died three months after we got there."

A fist closed around Kim's heart. "Oh. I'm sorry, Mark." Not till then did she realize how alone Mark was and had been for years. She wondered if telling him about her own mother would help ease his burden.

No. Best to turn the conversation onto a more cheerful path. "So, how did you end up a lawyer?"

He rubbed his jaw, thinking. "I kicked around Denver for a year, which was long enough to teach me there were no magic doors like the ones Miriam and I had dreamed about. The only way I was going to achieve anything was to go to school and actually work at becoming something."

Kim bit her lip, wondering what "kicked around Denver" meant. Homeless at eighteen, without relatives or friends to help, his life must have been unspeakably harsh.

"How were you able to afford school?"

"The usual way a kid with no money does. State school, financial aid, work."

Kim exhaled a long slow breath. "Well, you certainly have reason to be proud of yourself. Look what you've achieved."

"Yes." He gazed into the distance. Strangely, a frown gathered across his brow, a frown Kim longed to ease away with her fingers. Or a kiss.

She huddled into his jacket, frightened by the depth of affection she was feeling for this man.

"Well, that was a long answer to a simple question, wasn't it?"

Kim blinked. "I... What was the question?"

"The one about your arrest tonight and why I'm not angry. For one thing, it wasn't your fault, and for another you've been working so hard any idiot can see that whatever's behind it is pretty damn important to you. I have to tell you, kitten, I wasn't prepared for such industriousness."

"It's..." Kim wanted to tell him what she was working toward, but she knew he wouldn't understand. "It's..." she tried again. He reached over and brushed a wayward curl off her cheek. She turned to look at him, and trust flooded her heart. "I want to go to school."

Mark tilted his head. "Really?" Tilted it the other way. "Well, I'll be..." And then he chuckled. "That's wonderful, Kim. Really wonderful. What do you want to study?"

Kim gulped. She'd never found a way of saying this without having people laugh. "It's not a course of study so much as it is training."

"Ah." He nodded, still open and accepting. And waiting.

"I'm not sure if you're aware there's an increasing need for quality child care..."

"Oh, I know. With so many mothers working these days, day-care centers..."

She squinched her eyes. "That's not exactly the sort of situation... You see..." There was no easy way to explain. "I want to go to nanny school," she finally just blurted.

She waited for the guffaw, for the "What the hell is nanny school?" But all she heard was the spring wind rustling the dry winter grasses alongside the road.

"That's very interesting," Mark said. "That's one of the most novel ideas I've heard in a long time." Kim's jaw dropped in surprise.

He wagged a finger. "Now I get it, all the books on child care..." His eyes brightened as if he'd positioned an important piece of a puzzle. "But is it really necessary to go to school to become a nanny?"

"To become a *certified* nanny, yes. Certified nannies are, well, an elite group. Placement agencies can't find them fast enough. They're a lot different from au pairs, who are basically just foreign students who live in with a family for a year and baby-sit. A nanny is trained in child development, first aid—gosh, all sorts of things—how to shop for children's clothes, mending, even etiquette. But we don't do housework," she finished on a definitive note.

He laughed. "How's the money?"

"Okay. If you're certified. Then you have some clout and can demand benefits like medical coverage."

"And you get free room and board."

"Right, that, too. Of course, location makes a difference. As you'd expect, New York nannies are the highest paid."

Mark's attention sharpened. "And where exactly is this training school? Back in New York?"

"Yes, there's one there. But there are lots of others."

He hesitated. "In Colorado?"

Kim nodded. "I've already requested an application from the community college at Fort Morgan."

"You've really looked into this, haven't you?"

"Well, of course."

"Hmm. I'm surprised Miriam didn't tell me. Is this a new notion? Haven't you had a chance to tell her?"

"Oh, she knows." The joy of sharing her dream suddenly paled. Miriam had always known.

"I'm still a little confused, Kim. Are you working for tuition?"

"Yes." Too late she realized her mistake.

"But why? Why not just get on with it?"

Kim was at a loss. She didn't want to talk about tuition, didn't want to get into her fear that Miriam might renege on her promise to pay. And she certainly didn't want to get into the fact that Miriam controlled all the finances. Such talk would invariably lead Mark to see a side of his sister Kim preferred to keep hidden. "I will," she said evasively, "when Miriam gets here. I'm just waiting for us to get settled." She glanced at the clock on the dash. "Mark, it's awfully late."

He drew up his shoulders with a resolute sigh. "Yes." And dismissing the subject, he put the car in motion.

Kim was relieved. Sitting here with Mark had been magical, and even if it was only an isolated bubble in time, she wanted to remember the interlude untainted.

CHAPTER SIX

MARK DROVE TO WORK in a distracted state the next morning. Kim was turning into a prism with too many facets. A nanny? He supposed it was as good a dream as any.

What bothered him was not so much the dream but the fact that it was so clearly thought out. Why hadn't Miriam mentioned it to him, instead of implying Kim drifted from job to job? Mark drummed his fingers on the steering wheel and scowled. Maybe Kim *had* spent the past few years drifting and Miriam was justifiably skeptical of her claims of having finally found direction. Sure, that was probably it.

But that still didn't explain Kim's working so hard for tuition or her request that he not charge her room and board. And it definitely didn't explain the utter surprise he'd seen in her eyes the few times he'd helped her.

Mark stifled a yawn as he pulled into the parking area at work. He hadn't slept well the previous night. His mind had been too active, turning over these perplexities.

He cut the engine and stared at the heat-shimmer rising off the hood. He didn't like thinking about Kim so much. At work he was often tired and distracted. Not that anyone noticed. His performance seemed to remain impeccable. But *he* knew. Kim had become an unshakable presence he carried with him through his day.

What was worse, she seemed to be having an effect on his attitude. He was at a loss to explain it, but Kim was like a touchstone that had dropped into his life, causing him to test the value of everything he did. Lately he found himself rethinking his goals and ambitions, reexamining his dealings with colleagues and clients. He was even questioning his relationship with Suzanne. He wasn't in love with her, so why was he seeing her?

The situation wasn't good. It was causing him to do things that weren't in his best interest—such as arguing with Milton Barnes. He didn't like Barnes, and the creep had gotten what he deserved. Yet Mark couldn't help wondering, if Kim hadn't been involved...

And now there was this little matter of her arrest. He could only imagine how that would go over if the partners ever found out.

Mark closed his tired eyes. Kim was definitely a liability. In two short weeks she seemed to have halted the forward momentum of his life. He should've let her move out to that women's shelter when he'd had the chance.

And yet... what he remembered most clearly about Kim was the peace he'd felt last night sitting with her in his car, the feel of her in his arms, her warmth and softness. When they were alone like that, the rest of the world dropped away, and she became, not a liability, but a blinding fascination.

Mark shook his head to free himself of her image. It was a bad situation, but not one he couldn't remedy. And he would. He'd struggled too hard to get where he was. He wasn't about to slide back. He opened his car door, determined to put Kim out of his mind and to focus again on work.

Mark's secretary greeted him with an uncharacteristic dive into her typing.

" 'Morning, Willie."

She paused just long enough to say, "They want to see you. Brightman's office."

Mark felt a kick of adrenaline. Had the partners arrived at a decision regarding his promotion? "When?"

"Right now." Her eyes never left her work.

Mark put his briefcase in his office and hurried across the reception area to Brightman's office. "You wanted to see me?"

Three pairs of eyes speared into him. "Sit down, Mark," Bill Fuller ordered.

He remained standing. "What's the matter?"

With a disgusted huff, Ed Brightman flicked open the morning paper across his desk. Without even looking, Mark knew what was there. The floor seemed to dissolve from under his feet.

"It was quite a night," he quipped nonetheless, wanting to wring the reporter Lenox's neck.

"Indeed," Geoff Collins intoned dourly.

Mark picked up the paper and read the caption beneath the picture: "City attorney Mark Johnson escorts his stepniece—" Mark groaned "—Kim Wade, from police station following last night's raid of the Blue Lantern. Ms. Wade is a waitress at the restaurant." Then he skimmed the article that accompanied the picture.

The silence in the room was suffocating. "All right. Get it over with," Mark finally said. "You're obviously not jumping for joy over this."

"Damn right we're not." Brightman's face turned an alarming shade of fuchsia. "Mark, you know we can't put up with this sort of scandal."

Mark feared his own coloring was getting rather alarming, too. "What scandal? The article clearly explains that the raid was wholesale and that the majority of the employees were innocent."

"Sure, but most people don't bother reading entire articles. They read a couple of paragraphs, look at a photograph and jump to conclusions from there. Lord almighty, Mark, what's happened to your good sense? A month ago you wouldn't have been caught dead with a woman dressed like that, let alone allowed your picture to be taken with her.''

Mark's chest heaved. He wanted to grab Brightman's impeccable lapels and call him a supercilious prig. But he counted to ten and finally conceded that the partners were probably right about the image he and Kim presented. Reputations these days were based on nothing more substantial than flashing impressions and sound bytes.

"You did notice that the firm's name wasn't mentioned,'' he said.

"We know that,'' Fuller replied. "And we're thankful for small favors. But, Mark . . .'' He shook his head gravely.

"How long's that girl going to be with you?'' Brightman inquired.

"I don't know.'' Mark's steady gaze challenged.

"Well, make sure she keeps a low profile, you hear?''

Mark didn't want to feel angry. They were right, they were right. But the truth was, he was furious.

"Okay. That's all we have to say on the matter,'' Ed Brightman said. "In the short time you've been with us, you've become one of the firm's most valuable assets, so we're letting you off easy. Just you make sure it never happens again.''

Mark bit back his resentment and headed for the door.

"Oh, one more thing. The new incorporation papers we're handling for Milton Barnes?''

"You mean the papers Stu is handling,'' Mark corrected.

"Yes, well, we'd like you to get in on it, too. You know, oversee the fine points?'' Brightman didn't wait for a response. "One o'clock in the conference room.''

Mark swore all the way back to his office. Get in on it? Oversee the fine points? Who did they think they were kidding? Everybody in the firm knew Zambroski was in over his head and needed someone to throw him a lifeline.

Mark tried to contain his anger. He got through his mail, two morning appointments, and a foot-high stack of bureaucratic garbage. But at eleven he was angrier than ever.

"Hey, nice picture, Mark," Stu sneered, poking his head into Mark's office and waving a copy of the morning paper.

That did it! "Tell the unholy trinity I've gone home sick," he told his secretary on his way past her desk.

KIM AWOKE to the incessant ring of the doorbell. She shook her head to clear the cobwebs. Her clock read ten thirty-two. She threw on her robe, mashed her exuberant hair and ran for the stairs. A peek out the window revealed Suzanne's silvery-gray Mercedes parked at the curb. Kim's heart sank.

"Well, it's about time," the woman snapped, striding in.

"Is there something I can do for you?" Kim closed her robe and tightened the belt, aware that her nightshirt sported a picture of Bugs Bunny. Somehow Suzanne didn't strike her as a Bugs Bunny fan.

Suzanne pulled off her black leather gloves, one finger at a time. "I don't suppose you've seen today's paper yet?"

Kim squinted against the sharp morning light. She hadn't even seen the bathroom mirror yet. "Why? What's in..." She didn't have to finish the question. Or hear the answer. "Oh, no. They didn't."

Suzanne whipped out a newspaper from somewhere within her cape. Like a magician, Kim thought.

"You look precious," Suzanne drawled, thrusting the paper into Kim's midsection.

Kim stared at the photo and wanted to die. She hadn't realized she had so much cleavage! And Mark—Mark had his arm around her shoulder, an intimacy she hadn't been aware of until this moment.

Kim passed a shaky hand over her eyes. "Well, at least they spelled our names right."

Suzanne shook her head as if she were trying to communicate with a moron. "Do you have any idea how damaging this is going to be to Mark's career?"

Kim gulped. "No, I really don't. What's wrong with a guy coming to pick up his . . . a relative?"

"Who's just been arrested in a vice raid and is wearing a postage stamp? Gee, let me guess." Her sarcasm was grinding.

"I guess this isn't going to sit well with the people he works for."

"It isn't just them." Suzanne sighed wearily. "It's clients. It's our competitors. It's everybody. To say nothing about what you've done to Mark's future in politics."

Kim felt the color drain from her face. "Politics?"

Suzanne yanked open the door. "Do us all a favor, honey. Get out of Mark's life. I still can't figure out what you're doing here, anyway, and frankly I'm beginning to wonder just who the devil you are." She stormed off, her heels punishing the brick wall.

Kim picked up the paper, which Suzanne had thrown to the floor, and on rubbery legs tottered to the couch. Good Lord, what had she done to Mark now? But no sooner had she begun to read the article than the phone rang.

"Hello?"

"Kim Wade?" a male voice inquired.

She hesitated, wary. "Yes."

"Joe Hansen from the—"

Kim slammed down the phone before she had a chance to hear the name of the paper. Trembling, she returned to the sofa but got only halfway through the article when the phone rang again. This call came from the personnel manager at the department store where she worked. He'd seen the article and, much to her relief, laughed off the whole incident.

"You can't imagine how much I appreciate your sense of fairness." Kim's voice quavered. "I honestly thought you were calling to fire me."

"For what? Working another job? Kim, don't be absurd. I'm only calling to say relax, I realize you've probably been having a hell of a day, and I'd like to take you out. Dinner maybe. Someplace nice and quiet where nobody'll be pointing a finger."

Kim's face dropped. "I . . ." Her voice croaked, then anger gave her impetus. "I'm sorry, but I'm unavailable for dinner this evening. I'm also unavailable for work today— and every other day, too. In fact, you can take your crummy job and . . . and do you-know-what with it." She slammed down the receiver again, crumpled into Mark's desk chair and cradled her head on her folded arms.

"Well, I'm glad I'm not whoever that was."

Kim's head shot up. Mark was standing in the doorway, his suit jacket slung over his shoulder. He was smiling one of his bone-melting, heart-stopping smiles, and for a moment the world stood still.

"Mark, sit down. Something awful has come of that incident last night."

"Oh. You've heard."

She blinked in surprise. "All morning. You?"

He answered with an eloquent roll of his eyes.

"Oh, Mark, I'm so sorry."

He walked over and, sitting on the corner of the desk, placed a finger on her lips. "What've we got for lunch?"

"But, Mark—"

"I don't want to hear it."

Kim became painfully aware she was still in her bathrobe and big fuzzy slippers. "How does a bacon-lettuce-and-tomato sound?"

"Like heaven." He stood up, gripped her hand and headed for the kitchen. His touch caused a tingling right down to her toes.

"Hey, what are you doing home at this hour?"

"I'm starting the weekend early." He tossed his jacket over a kitchen chair and, as if they were coconspirators, winked at her.

As she was opening the refrigerator, the phone rang again. Kim looked at Mark. He looked at her.

"Let the machine answer it," he said.

"Gladly." Kim proceeded to arrange bacon strips on a microwave tray, while Mark carefully sliced a tomato.

The caller was Mark's secretary, wondering if he was sure he wouldn't be back by one. Mark didn't bat an eye.

They ate to the sound of the phone ringing twice more, both callers hanging up when they realized they'd have to talk to a machine.

Mark brushed the last toast crumbs off his hands, looked across the table and quite resolutely announced, "Kim, it's time I introduced you to the wonderful world of Colorado skiing."

Her eyes snapped wide open. "Skiing? Where? When?" She was also going to ask why, but she thought she already knew the answer.

"Breckenridge. We can leave today as soon as we're packed."

"You aren't serious. Are you?"

In answer he gathered up their lunch things and practically threw them into the dishwasher as if the trip were already under way.

Kim sat stunned, watching him. "There's one small problem, Mark. No, two. Wait. Three."

He arched one eyebrow as he wiped down the cutting board.

"I've never been on skis in my life."

"Yeah, so you'll take a lesson. What's the next problem?"

"I have no equipment, no clothes or anything."

"Hmm." He checked his watch. "So we'll start a couple of hours later than planned. What's the third problem?" This man was accepting nothing as a hurdle.

"I don't want to spend my money on anything as frivolous as skiing."

Mark came over and hauled her out of her chair. "You're my guest. You're not supposed to pay. Now, let's get moving. Breckenridge is a good three hours away, and we have things to do before we even hit the road."

"Mark, I can't. You've done too much already." She grew uncomfortably aware of their closeness.

"I'm doing this as much for myself as for you, lady. This whole thing's ridiculous, and ordinarily I'd stick around to tell everyone involved what jackasses they're being, but right now I can't be bothered. Let's go and enjoy ourselves. We'll hit the slopes, do the swingin' singles scene." His smile warmed. "By the time we get back Sunday night, I'm sure everything will've blown over. Come on," he coaxed seductively. "It's time you really saw Colorado."

"Well, since I'm unemployed, anyway..." She groaned, realizing she'd have to resume the job hunt all over again on Monday. "What do we do first?"

He gave her a quick laughing hug. "Strap on your shopping shoes, kitten. We're going for a ride.

"LET'S GET YOUR equipment first," Mark suggested, steering Kim toward the ski-rental area at the rear of a pricey sporting-goods shop. On the way he casually plucked a pair of socks off a display rack. "Here. You'll need these to get a good fit."

The ordeal of outfitting her took forever. At least that's how it felt. But Mark never once looked restless or impatient. In fact, as he supervised the tension adjustment on her bindings, she realized he was actually enjoying himself.

Leaving her equipment by the cash register, they ventured into the clothing department where they flipped through the bright racks, Mark pulling out ski suits faster than she could think. He held one up beside her, his eyes measuring her in a manner that brought heat to her cheeks.

"I like the color on you." The suit was daffodil yellow with a navy racing stripe down the side. "Think size six will do?"

She nodded, amazed, and wondered just how much shopping he did for women. "I'd better try it on to be sure."

"Here, take this sweater, too. And these thermals. And a turtleneck . . ."

When she emerged from the dressing room, he was tumbling over stacks of colorful knit hats. The tumbling stopped, and so did he. His movement. His breathing. Kim's mouth was as dry as cotton as she endured his inspection. Her heart was hammering frantically.

Which was crazy, she thought. As crazy as the hot sweep of his eyes and the approval in his slow easy smile. Something had begun to go wrong with their relationship at least a week ago. Now it was so far off course, she feared nothing could get it back on.

His gaze swept the bright yellow outfit again. "Yes," he said. Just one word, but it spoke volumes to her.

By the time they returned to the house, Kim was dazed. She'd agreed to this shopping spree thinking that eventually she'd repay him, but unless she hit a lottery, "eventually" was going to be a very long time. Oddly, the trip seemed to energize Mark. He bounded up the stairs, dumped the parcels on her bed, then dashed across the hall to pack his bag.

"Why are we rushing?" Kim panted, as he hurried her out to the Cherokee. They'd accomplished what appeared a herculean task, and it was still only three-fifteen.

"I don't want to be driving in the dark."

"Oh." She weighed his concern against the fact that he was an excellent driver. "What kind of roads will we be traveling?"

"The kind that take your breath away. I don't want you to miss a mile."

As they headed out of the city, Kim felt indescribably content. No one had ever done as much for her as Mark had in just these past two weeks. But it wasn't the cost of the clothes that touched her, or the glamour of this trip. What got to her were the small intangibles. Like his hurrying so that *she* could enjoy the ride. Like his taking her nanny dream seriously...and not once, not once mentioning her waitressing uniform.

Mark was a gentleman of the first order, and it was probably only because she'd never met one before, Kim decided, that she was falling in love with him.

CHAPTER SEVEN

MARK DOWNSHIFTED as the twisting two-lane highway climbed even higher.

"There go the ears again." Beside him, Kim tilted her head and jiggled her ear like a waterlogged swimmer. Mark's own ears had been popping for miles.

"Oh, Mark!" Kim clutched his forearm.

He pulled to the side of the road, gazing not at the panorama that had just opened out, but at Kim's fresh awestruck expression.

"Mark! I've never seen anything so beautiful!"

"We just came over Wilkerson Pass. Gets me everytime, too."

"Wilkerson Pass," she repeated. Then she laughed softly. "We've been on the road for at least an hour, and all that time I thought the scenery couldn't get any better."

They got out and walked to the crusty snow plowed to the side of the road. Wilkerson Pass was more than 9,000 feet high, and from that vantage point they gazed across countless miles of snow-swept plateau toward an endless rampart of mountains in the distance. The late afternoon sun cast a white-gold brilliance over the scene that was dazzling.

"Nothing in my life has prepared me for this."

Mark glanced at Kim's solemn profile and drew deep satisfaction from her pleasure.

He still couldn't believe he was here, couldn't believe he'd walked off the job, leaving Zambroski to fend for himself.

Mark knew he should be concerned. The esteemed partners were probably in a lather by now. He should be worried.

But the truth was, he couldn't scare up a worry to save his life. Right now he was too busy with other emotions, like the joy he was feeling and the sense of freedom.

"Mark." Kim touched his arm. "Listen."

He did. "I don't hear anything."

"Precisely," she whispered.

Yes, it *was* silent, utterly and completely. Here in the Rockies, the world was filled with an enormity of silence, blanketing everything Mark could see, for hundreds of miles around.

No, not blanketing, he thought, feeling his heart sing with peace. The silence was really a loud rejoicing.

Mark heard Kim sniff. "Cold air," she quickly explained. "It bothers the sinuses."

Mark wasn't fooled. He moved closer and wrapped her hand in his. Like him, she'd left her gloves in the car and her fingers were cold.

He let her drink in her fill of the view without saying anything to break the spell. Finally she turned and smiled her readiness to continue the journey.

They stopped for an early-evening meal in a small town called Fairplay. They were only twenty miles from their destination, but Mark had heard Kim's stomach growling, and he knew the food at the historic Fairplay Hotel would be good.

"Penny for your thoughts," he asked as he tucked into the hearty vegetable soup they'd both ordered. He'd been watching Kim covertly from the moment they'd stepped into the place. His pleasure deepened as she blushed.

"I'm sorry. You must think I'm such a yokel, but I've never traveled, Mark, and I'm afraid I'm acting like a gawking tourist."

Holding her gaze captive within his, he slowly shook his head. "You're looking at things with fresh eyes, that's all, and I'm having the time of my life coming along for the ride. It's been too long..." When had he lost his zest for life? he wondered. And why was it all flooding back now?

"So, what do you think of the place?"

She sighed, smiling dreamily. "If Wyatt Earp walked through those doors right now, I wouldn't even blink. I love that bar. Cowboys should be lined up at it instead of guys in Nikes. And I love those Victorian light fixtures and that upright piano. But the thing I'll remember most, I think, is the squeak of the floorboards. More than anything else, that squeak transports me to another era. Have you ever noticed that? How something minor like the scent of furniture polish or the angle of sunlight through...?" She paused, becoming aware of his steady smiling gaze. "What? Why are you laughing?" she asked, bristling with defensiveness. "Am I talking too much?"

"Not laughing, Kim. Just enjoying the ride."

By the time they reached Breckenridge, darkness had fallen. The ski trails, spread across the three huge mountains that towered over the town, were now deserted and still, but the après-ski scene was just coming to life.

Mark had called ahead and reserved two rooms at a slopeside resort hotel. After checking in, he and Kim took the elevator up to their rooms. Kim was directly across the hall from him, and they opened their doors so they could talk as they unpacked. Mark chuckled. She got such a kick out of things he'd come to take for granted, simple things like the feel of plush carpeting under bare feet and the free toiletries in the bath.

"Done," she announced, standing on his threshold with an eager smile. It was Friday night and the place was filling fast with weekend vacationers. Music was thrumming from a lounge somewhere below.

"Me, too. Are you awake enough to go downstairs for a drink?"

"Sure."

They followed the music to its source, a crowded lounge on the main floor. A band was playing country rock, and the people on the dance floor seemed at least three drinks ahead of them. They found two seats at an already occupied table.

"What'll you have?" Mark had to lean close to be heard.

"Hmm. I think . . . a martini."

"A martini?" Mark asked as the waitress walked off.

"I've never had one before, and since this seems to be a weekend for doing new things..." Kim glanced away, color staining her cheeks.

Mark was starting to feel mighty uneasy, too. This probably wasn't right, this being here alone with Kim.

Their drinks arrived. "Better nurse that thing, Kimberly," Mark warned in his most avuncular tone.

She smirked. "Yes, sir."

The other people sitting at their table were young, in their twenties. Their skin glowed from a day of skiing.

"Hi." One of the young men smiled at Kim. He'd been staring at her since she'd sat down.

Her hesitant smile persuaded Mark to lean toward her ear. "It's okay. You can say hi back."

She did, and Mark fought down a twinge of displeasure, reminding himself that here was the reason for this trip. Not only did Kim need a break from the insanity created by that newspaper photo, but she needed to meet people her own age and cut loose. He didn't imagine she'd done much of that in the past.

When the young man asked Mark if he minded his dancing with Kim, Mark jumped at the opportunity to explain they weren't together. "Kim's my niece," he said. But it was becoming increasingly difficult to get the word out, and he knew his paltry attempt to throw up fences wasn't going to work much longer.

IF KIM COULD PICK one day in her entire life to save in a magic bottle, a day she could relive anytime she wished, it would be this one, she thought the next evening, as she shampooed her hair under the hot tingling shower. Today she had actually learned to ski!

Not well, of course. But she'd mastered the snowplow, she'd learned to get on and off lifts without falling, and Mark claimed he'd never known anyone to make such progress in one day. At the rate she was going, he said, she'd be paralleling in no time.

He was an advanced skier himself, and while she'd taken her lesson this morning, he'd ventured off on his own. When he'd rejoined her, his hair had been matted and his face was ruddy from the bite of the wind.

''Where have you been?'' she'd asked.

''The top of the world, Kim. The very top.'' He'd gestured toward the wide open bowls above the timberline. From where she'd stood, the few adventurous skiers up there had been hard to discern, mere dots barely moving across the sun-dazzled snow.

''Powder skiing,'' Mark had explained. ''Nothing else like it on earth. One of these days, I'll have to take you with me.'' Kim's heart still somersaulted when she remembered his invitation.

For the rest of the day he'd stayed with her. Kim rinsed the suds from her hair and laughed aloud as images flashed across her mind. Mark skiing backward, directly in front of her, talking her through her moves. Mark getting bowled over as she'd lurched out of control—and grabbed his head for support!

And then there was that unplanned trip into the woods. Luckily she hadn't hit any trees, but her plight had still been dire. She hadn't realized how dire until she'd tried to move. Her skis and heavy boots had plowed so deep beneath the soft unpacked snow that her legs felt as though they'd been cast in cement.

Mark had arrived in an instant. "Are you all right?"

"I think so. Except I'm stuck." Suddenly her predicament had struck her as terribly funny. Lying there, snow down her back, hat lost and poles askew, she'd begun to laugh.

"What did you say?" He'd looked so grave, even upside down.

"I'm stuck. Afraid you're going to have to come to the rescue again, Sir Knight."

"Oh, Kim." The tenderness in his voice had made her heart sing. "Okay, let me take off my skis, or both of us'll need rescuing."

Getting her out of the woods had become a full-blown comedy. Mark had been forced to burrow through thigh-deep snow, searching tactilely for her skis. One slid out easily, but the other pivoted up and snagged in the twiggy pine branches over her head.

Finally, finally, he'd freed her, but they were both puffing from the deceptively difficult task. They'd collapsed on the edge of the hard-packed trail, weak with laughter.

A member of the ski patrol had come by and asked if they were all right. Kim had tried to sober up but failed, leaving Mark to answer for them.

"Yes, we're fine, thank you," he'd said with a remarkable amount of dignity, just before succumbing to another bout of laughter.

Yes, the day had been perfect, Kim thought, drying herself off with a thick white towel. A sky so blue it seemed unreal, air as light as champagne . . . and Mark, Mark looking more handsome than any man had a right to look.

They'd left the slopes around four and driven into the center of town where they'd spent an hour browsing through shops and admiring the authentic Victorian architecture of the buildings. Now, she was famished. The exercise and fresh air had given her an appetite. Quickly she dried her hair and dressed.

"Do I look okay?" she asked when she met Mark out in the hall.

"Oh, mercy!" He spoke so low he probably intended the remark to go unheard.

But Kim caught it clearly enough. Her heart plummeted. She gave her jeans and blouse an uncertain check. She'd *thought* she looked okay. Was it the blouse? Didn't it go with the jeans? It was sort of dressy—cream silk, with slightly padded shoulders and a low V-necked collar. Too dressy? she worried.

"What? What's this 'oh mercy' business? What do you expect me to wear? I didn't pack a whole lot of stuff, you know."

Mark smiled one of his warm-as-molasses smiles, put his arm around her and turned her to face a framed oval mirror. Its shape echoed that of a dozen old sepia portraits hanging along the corridor, portraits unearthed from dusty attics, no doubt.

"Do you ever stop being defensive long enough to look at yourself?" He held her against him with one arm while his free hand cupped her jaw and tilted her face toward the mirror. "Look at yourself, Kim," he commanded.

She did, but nothing was registering. Suddenly the only thing she was aware of was the heat and hardness of Mark's body pressed along the length of her own.

"You look sensational." He delivered each word with distinct emphasis.

She tried to look at herself again, but what she found in the mirror was not Kim Wade but a couple, a couple whose eyes were bright and whose bodies were linked. For one crazy moment, they appeared to be another of the antique portraits that hung on the wall, frozen in time.

Mark's smile faded and she'd have sworn a matching awareness rose through him. He let her go. "So, where would you like to eat?"

She pulled in a shuddery breath. "It doesn't matter." As long as they were with other people, and soon.

With a light hand at her waist, he started toward the elevator. "Then you won't mind that I've already made reservations here."

"No. S-sounds nice."

Once they reached the lobby, Mark steered her through an open arch.

"Oh, my," Kim whispered as she peeked into an intimate firelit room. A pianist was playing somewhere in the flickering shadows.

With his hand ever present at her waist, they followed the hostess to a candlelit table set within a bay of windows. A special table, it seemed, for it not only afforded a view of the moon-washed slopes but also allowed them to see the fire perfectly, even hear the logs hissing on the grate.

"Enjoy your meal." The hostess smiled. Kim wondered if she thought they were a couple.

"Are we skiing again tomorrow?" She opened her menu.

"If you'd like. Why?"

"Just wondering if I should order pasta. You know, energy food."

Mark grinned. "Order anything you like."

Kim was about to ask what time he planned to set out for home, but somehow the words wouldn't come. She wanted this weekend to go on forever.

"Then I'll have the tortellini with Alfredo sauce," she said. Mark ordered prime rib. They shared a carafe of wine.

As they ate, they relived their day, the runs they'd made, the condition of the snow. Quite often they found themselves laughing again.

"It's funny, but I still have the sensation I'm on skis," Kim said, spearing an olive from her salad. "My feet are tingling, and when I close my eyes I feel as if I'm gliding."

"Are you sure it's not another Rocky Mountain high?"

Kim stared at Mark across the candlelight and knew that if anything was making her dizzy these days, it wasn't the altitude.

Their meals were superbly prepared, and they relished each bite. It seemed they'd both rediscovered their taste buds on this brief weekend escape.

But inevitably, as they sipped their after-dinner coffee, Kim thought again about returning to Colorado Springs. "Wouldn't it be lovely if..."

"If what?"

"Nothing."

"If we didn't have to go back?"

She glanced away and nodded.

"This has been nice, hasn't it?" He reached across the table and covered her hand with his. Kim reeled in confusion. His touch was sending tremors up her arm and shaking her to her roots. Should she pull away? Ask what he was doing?

Nervously she met his gaze. It was steady, direct and waiting, waiting for the slightest sign of withdrawal from her. He'd held her hand before, had even hugged her on occasion. But this touch was different. She didn't move, hardly even dared to breathe. Then, feeling as if she were stepping into space, she turned her hand over and her palm met his in hot intoxicating intimacy.

A smile entered his eyes. "Would you care to dance?"

The piano player had moved into a medley of old tunes, lovely danceable pieces from the thirties and forties, and several couples were already out on the floor.

Kim stood up, wondering if her legs would bear her weight. She felt fragile, light, a butterfly not sure where to settle, where to touch down, as Mark turned to take her in his arms. And then it just happened. He pulled her toward him, one arm firm around her waist, the other tucking her against his racing heart. Until now, they could have made excuses for their occasional shows of affection, but dancing was something else again, especially the kind of dancing that was promised in his eyes.

Was she even drawing breath? she wondered, as they began to sway. She didn't know. In Mark's arms she lost awareness of everything except him. She watched him continue to watch her for signs of resistance, and when she gave none, he gathered her closer still. His breath kissed her hair, and her heartbeat quickened.

With a shuddering sigh, Kim surrendered to the attraction she'd felt from the moment they'd met. She let herself snuggle into the warm crook of his shoulder, inviting his cheek to caress her temple.

They'd both surrendered. There was no way either of them could rationalize what was happening between them tonight. There were bound to be consequences, repercussions felt all the way back to Colorado Springs, but Kim didn't want to think about them now. Mark was moving his hand over her back in a slow sinuous caress; his head turned a fraction so that his slightly parted lips were at her temple—and Kim's powers of reasoning completely disintegrated. *This* was all that mattered. This glorious feeling. This one perfect day.

Here, away from the city, they didn't have to worry about superimposed roles or proper image. They were free to be themselves, to follow their natural instincts. And this felt totally right.

The tune ended, but the pianist, with a smooth transition, moved immediately into another. Mark lifted his head, just enough to gaze into her eyes, which at the moment felt too heavy-lidded to open. "One more?"

Kim's lips parted to answer, and he tipped his head forward. *He's going to kiss me,* she thought, her heart thumping at an unholy rate. But he didn't. His mouth merely lifted at one corner before he folded her close again.

Kim wouldn't have blamed him if he had. The heat they were generating was fiercer than the flames dancing on the grate. When Mark moved his hand under her hair and began a soft stroking of her neck, Kim felt a bead of sweat trickle between her breasts.

The number they swayed to now was another old song—soft, lyrical, romantic. Gershwin, she thought vaguely. One more minute of this, and she feared she'd float clear off the floor.

"I think I have to sit down, Kim." Mark's whisper rasped against her ear.

She shivered. "Why? What's the matter?"

"You. You're what's the matter." He tried to make light of the situation, but the desire that smoldered in his eyes was all business.

With his arm draping her shoulders and hers circling his waist, they returned to their table no longer the tenuously related friends they'd been during dinner. They'd crossed a threshold and returned now as lovers.

They sat and for a long stunned moment studied each other across the candle glow. Then, all in one movement, Mark groaned, shuddered and nervously rumpled his hair. "What the hell've we started here, Kim?"

She was as lost as he and could only shake her head.

"Will there be anything else?" The waitress's appearance seemed to startle Mark as much as it did Kim. She'd begun to think they were the only two people left on the planet.

Mark glanced at Kim and she shook her head. "Just the check," he replied.

They filled the elevator ride with overanimated chatter about wake-up calls, breakfast and checkout time, but Kim suspected Mark was as distracted as she.

Where would this day end? she wondered in mounting anticipation. With a kiss? With more? Or was Mark already regretting having gone this far?

He remained with her while she dug out her room key from her purse, but as the door swung in, she braced herself for a brusque good-night, if that was the course he decided to take.

Instead, he walked past her into the room and switched on the bedside lamp. "I know we're both tired," he said, as if to ease any fears she might have that he was staying. "We've had a full day..." He moved toward the door, which had remained slightly open. "I just wanted to make sure the room was okay."

"No boogeymen? No dragons under the bed?"

He glanced away, shrugging, and on a wave of insight Kim realized that, in his typically chivalrous way, Mark really had wanted to make sure she was safe.

"You're a very nice man, Mark Johnson." She stepped toward him and touched his cheek. A shudder ran through him. He closed his eyes and turned his lips to her palm.

A moment later, he'd pulled her into his arms and was pressing her close, molding her to him, as if some iron band of control had snapped. "Oh, Kim...Kim, I'm sorry."

Kim wrapped her arms around his shoulders and stroked the silky hair that curled over his collar. "There's nothing to be sorry about."

"I've wanted to do this for so long."

She'd never been embraced with such fervor. Her heart ached with the joy of it. "Me, too. Oh, Mark..." She was still speaking his name when he pressed his lips to hers, and the ache swelled to a soaring.

She heard the door close and could only guess that he'd nudged it shut with his foot, because both his arms were still holding her tight. His mouth moved over hers as if the feel of it, the taste of it, was giving him sustenance. He moaned as she responded.

Kim had never known such need for a man before. So fast. So intense. But then, she'd never been with anyone like Mark. He was older, experienced and undoubtedly he knew exactly how to elicit such a response from a woman.

His hands, fingers spread, delved into her hair and held her head captive while their kiss deepened. A few boys from her past had tried to kiss her this way. Distasteful was how she remembered the experience. But this, what Mark was doing with the soft gentle darting of his tongue, was turning her body to a river of fire.

He felt her response. He had to, because she felt an answering one from him. He smoothed his hands down her back to her hips, caressing each curve and hollow on the way, as if he needed the feel of her, all of her, all at once.

And for the first time in her life, Kim was afraid she might give in and surrender all of herself. Which was crazy, a small voice inside her warned. She and Mark had only just begun their romantic journey. She'd always thought that when she made love, she and her partner would be married—or at least would've been dating a very long time. Commitment would be involved.

But what was blazing between her and Mark had nothing to do with that girlhood fantasy. The timing was off. Too hot. Too soon. They weren't ready. No—*she* wasn't ready. The volatility of the situation frightened her. That was the real issue here. Mark was undoubtedly used to enjoying far more than she knew how to give. If they went any further, she was afraid she wouldn't measure up.

"Mark." Pulling her head back, she gasped for breath. "Mark, we have to stop."

His frustration escaped on a ragged groan. "I know. I'm sorry. I never meant for this to happen." Still, he seemed unable to heed his own words. He kissed her again, deeply, lingeringly.

"Mark!" She pressed her palms to his chest.

"Yes. Yes, of course." Closing his eyes, he brought his forehead to rest against hers and breathed deeply. Finally he stepped away, determinedly looking aside. "You're right."

Kim wasn't sure she agreed. Every inch of her ached to join him again and follow the promise in his touch.

He paced to the night-dark window. "How would we ever explain this to Miriam?" he asked, not having a clue what Kim's objections had been.

"Miriam?" The name hit like a cold splash of reality.

"Hmm. She sent you out here for me to look after you. Instead, I betray her trust and start messing around. What kind of person does that make me?"

Kim clutched her arms, suddenly feeling cold and empty. "Messing around? Is that how you define what happened just now?" She was afraid her voice wobbled.

He turned from the window. "Sorry. That came out harsher than intended." He looked slightly confused. He jammed his hands into his pockets and paced, hunched with silent burdens. "You have to agree, though, it is a sticky situation. I can't imagine how we'll explain it to her. Besides, it's more than just Miriam." He paused, his eyes bleak. "Kim, how can we ever explain ourselves to the people I know back in Colorado Springs? Tell me that."

Kim groped for the chair she knew was behind her. "Of course, I should've known." She sat unsteadily. Mark was an up-and-coming lawyer in a prestigious firm. He had high aspirations and a girlfriend who was far more appropriate to his life-style.

"Bad enough I tried to pass you off as my niece and the newspaper caught me up on it." He resumed his pacing. "If we start showing up places as a couple now, people will think I lied on purpose to whitewash our living together. My integrity would be compromised."

Integrity, my foot! Kim was trembling, but she refused to give in to the stinging in her eyes.

"We can't let that happen," he said. "We simply have to get this thing under control and end it, here, tonight."

Even as he spoke, however, Kim felt the heat scintillating between them across a distance of at least ten feet, and she wondered just how a person went about getting feelings as volatile as theirs under control.

By getting angry, by getting tough—and retreating to a place deep inside that was safe and numb. Wasn't that how she'd handled other setbacks in her life?

She reminded herself that Mark didn't consider her important enough to risk tainting his image. He had career goals to reach, other people to please, and Kim Wade simply did not fit into the agenda. Worse than that, she messed it up! Didn't she always?

As she purposely dwelled on these thoughts, outwardly she grew more composed. When her anger really galvanized, she was smiling.

"No problem, Mark. The incident's already forgotten."

Mark's eyes narrowed. Her equanimity seemed to unbalance him. "Kim, what's wrong?" He came around the bed and stood before her.

"Nothing. I simply see your point. I agree. People would gossip. About our age difference, or how ill-suited we are, or the fact that we're vaguely related. And then there's that small matter of my recent arrest. They'd stomp all over you with that, wouldn't they? So, we'll just forget what happened and then there won't be any gossip."

"Kim, I never..." His scowl darkened. But a moment later he shrugged and admitted, "Good. I'm glad you agree."

"Good. I'm glad you're glad. Now, I think we both need some sleep, especially if we're still planning to ski tomorrow. We are, aren't we?" It was her way of asking if he could let the incident slide as easily as she had.

He stared at her for a long quiet moment. "Yes," he answered finally. "We'll ski." She'd given him exactly what he'd asked for, control over the situation, yet when he left her room, he looked more baffled than ever.

THAT NIGHT, before she went to sleep, Kim opened her journal and thought of all the things she'd done that day. She'd never learned so much, laughed so often or loved so deeply. She sat with her pen poised over the blank page for nearly fifteen minutes before finally deciding what to write. So much had happened, so much she wanted to record, yet when she closed the journal, only one brief line had come to mind. "There are no perfect days."

CHAPTER EIGHT

THE RADIO RECEPTION on the drive home was poor.

"Check the glove compartment. I usually keep a few tapes there."

Kim rummaged through the clutter and came up grinning. "Reba McEntire? The Gatlin Brothers?"

"What's so funny?"

"You. You're a closet country freak."

"Am not."

She pulled out another tape. "Ha! Tammy Wynette. Do the esteemed partners know about this?"

Mark grinned back at her. They were doing well today, he thought, very well, considering what had transpired the night before—though, in truth, Kim deserved most of the credit. He'd barely slept, worrying about their predicament, but this morning she'd met him for breakfast smiling, as if everything between them was perfectly normal. They'd spent the morning skiing, and not another word had been said about the passion that had ignited between them. He'd broached the subject once, asked rather clumsily if she was okay, but she'd tossed back her hair like an irritated colt and said she didn't want to talk about it. After that he'd pretended nothing had happened, too, and only occasionally did a sulky look steal into her eyes to remind him that something *had* happened and maybe she hadn't forgotten.

Their cordiality was an act worthy of an Oscar. He wondered how long it could last. Indefinitely, he hoped, because a relationship with Kim was simply untenable. How *would* he explain it to Miriam? How could she not see him as an opportunist, using Kim and their living arrangement to serve his needs? Considering Miriam's concern for Kim's welfare, she'd probably never forgive him. He wouldn't blame her, either.

And then there was that matter of his integrity—the niece/stepniece issue and whether he'd purposely lied to whitewash Kim's living with him. Not that he believed there *was* an issue. It was nobody's business who stayed at his house. He just didn't like the possibility of being thought duplicitous. Besides, he already had a relationship going, with Suzanne.

Mark grimaced. Funny, how Suzanne occurred to him last.

Somehow Kim had misconstrued his motives, though. She thought he was concerned people would gossip. And he hadn't corrected her. A frown tightened his brow. Why? Why hadn't he denied it? All morning he'd been assuring himself that he'd just been so relieved by her agreement to forget the incident in her room that he hadn't cared what she assumed. But now he had to wonder, if she *had* struck a nerve? *Did* he care what people thought? Did a part of him believe she might actually be detrimental to his career?

Kim popped a tape into the player and adjusted the volume. Mark tried to keep his attention on the road and not on the shimmer of her long auburn hair. Her hair won.

Damn! Kim might be young and slightly rough around the edges, but she was also the brightest, most lovely creature he'd ever met, and in her company he was happier than he'd been in a long time. And whether people gossiped or the partners disapproved meant so little to him right now his concern was practically negligible.

"Actually, I don't mind this music myself," she said. "It's sort of romantic, all those lyrics about men drinking themselves blind over women who've walked out on them."

Mark wondered if he should tell her how beautiful she looked. No one on the slopes had been able to hold a candle to her. The clothes had helped, but it was that smile...

She wasn't aware of her assets. Quite the opposite. She downplayed them with a disregard that bordered on an inferiority complex, and his withdrawal from her last night hadn't helped. He should tell her, to bolster her confidence. But how? How could he without stepping into dangerous territory again?

"Oh, look." Kim touched his shoulder with one hand and pointed with the other. He told himself to ignore the touch and the heat it was generating.

He looked past her. Two horses were cavorting across a field deep with snow. They seemed mythical in their grace, their chestnut coats gleaming in the sun.

All at once she seemed to become aware of touching him, jerking her hand back into her lap. A moment later, the pained look was in her eyes again. But then she tossed back her hair with cool indifference, dug out a book from her bag, and for the next fifteen minutes the only sound between them was the plaintive twanging from the tape player.

Mark drove on, becoming increasingly reflective. Kim was one tough cookie, all right.

"Mark, can we stop?" She swiveled against the constraints of her seat belt.

Mark slowed and pulled off the road. "Good idea. I need a stretch, too."

"No. Can we back up and check out that old house?" She was already slipping on her ski jacket.

He cast a doubtful look down the road but did as she'd asked. It was a relief to see her excited about something again.

"It's a real, bona fide log cabin, isn't it?" Her boots crunched the snow as she hurried across a small clearing.

"I guess." He was used to seeing places like this.

The cabin was small and dark, three rooms, two windows. The door was missing.

"Think anybody ever lived here?" she asked, stepping inside. She ran her hand along what remained of the white caulking plugged between two rough-hewn timbers.

"It's possible."

Her eyes sparkled. "I can't imagine it. These mountains might be beautiful, but they're also awfully scary. What did they think they were doing, settling way out here in the middle of nowhere?"

Mark sat on the worn wooden threshold, his knees jack-knifed. "Following a dream?"

It was a narrow doorway, and when she joined him, they almost touched. "What do you think their dream was? Gold? Silver?"

"Maybe. But I'd guess a ranch." Automatically, he lifted his arm toward her shoulder but caught himself just in time.

"As long as we're on the subject of dreams," he ventured cautiously, "tell me more about this nanny thing you've got your sights set on. I have to tell you, I'm curious as hell as to where you got the idea."

She was quiet a while. He understood. He didn't like people poking into his life, either.

"I got the idea years ago. When I was fifteen."

He was surprised she'd decided to answer him. And pleased. "Been a long time coming, hasn't it?"

"Hmm. My friends and I used to take the subway over to Manhattan sometimes, mostly Saturdays, but a couple of times we skipped school. They weren't the best of companions," she offered hesitantly. "But then, those weren't the best of times, either."

"Can you tell me about them, where you lived, who you lived with? I've never asked..."

She lowered her gaze. "I lived with my father in Brooklyn, same place, all my life. Not a neighborhood likely to be featured in *Better Homes*, I'm afraid. But it wasn't the worst, either," she hastened to add. "The house originally belonged to my grandmother, before she died and left it to Dad. A duplex. When I was little, she lived on the second floor, Dad and I on the first."

"Where was your mother during all this?"

Kim's gaze skittered across the wild open landscape, searching. She shrugged.

"What do you mean? You don't know?"

"She and Dad divorced when I was three. I haven't seen her since."

Mark lifted his arm and this time let it touch her, lightly. She didn't seem to notice. "How did you manage? Who took care of you?"

"My grandmother, until she died."

"Which was when?"

"I was nine."

Mark wanted to tighten his hold but didn't dare. "And after that?"

"I pretty much fended for myself. I had my father, of course..."

"But?"

She shrugged evasively. "Dad had what's politely called a drinking problem."

Mark felt his insides knotting. "Was it bad?"

"Bad enough. It finally got him killed."

"The accident—he was driving drunk?"

Kim blinked a few times, her only response.

"So, when did my sister waltz onto the scene?"

"Let's see... I was fifteen when Dad started seeing her. Right after the incident I started telling you about ages ago! Can I get on with it?"

"Sure. No more questions. You and your friends went over to Manhattan..."

"Yes. We had this thing about terrorizing the sales people at Saks." She smiled sadly. "Another thing we liked to do was sit on the edge of Central Park and make fun of the people coming and going from their apartments across Fifth Avenue, even the poor doormen.

"One particular day, though, I happened to notice two young women leave one of the poshier addresses, but I could tell they weren't wealthy themselves. They started coming toward us across the avenue pushing baby strollers..."

"Nannies?"

"Hmm. Though it took me a while to figure that out." Kim pressed the heels of her hands against her eyes.

"What did you do, Kim?" Mark suspected she was trying to blot out the recollection.

"I got up off the grass and approached them. But you need to get the whole picture, Mark. I had a cigarette hanging from one lip, I was dressed in ratty denim, chin to toe, and had a button pinned right here—" she touched her left breast "—that read Born to Be Wild."

Mark tried not to laugh but failed. "Sorry. It couldn't have been easy, with no one at home to guide you."

He watched her lift her chin, flick back her hair, and he sensed her life had been harder than he imagined—or she would ever let on.

"So, you approached the two girls?"

"Yes. All I wanted to do was ask them how a person got such a great baby-sitting job. I mean, *I* did baby-sitting. I was a damn good baby-sitter. But this looked like a different game entirely."

"Did they answer you?"

"Yes. At first one of them did. She said they weren't 'baby-sitters.' Boy, did she drag that word down. She said they lived in with families and took care of the children full-time.

"Well, I must've become pretty excited by that bit of news and started asking lots of questions, because they looked me over, looked at my friends, and they got this expression in their eyes I'll never forget."

Kim lowered her head to her arms, folded across her knee, and fell silent. Telling this story was draining her. Yet Mark wanted her to continue. He sensed she'd never told it to anyone before.

Finally she raised her head, eyes fixed boldly on the far horizon. "All I wanted was information. Their lives seemed so clean to me, so safe. *I* could push a baby carriage as well as they could. *I* could read bedtime stories. So, how did I get one of those jobs? How did I go about becoming part of one of those clean, safe families?"

Mark fought an urge to pull her against him. "What was the look you saw in their eyes, Kim?"

She heaved a sigh filled with remembered pain. "Fear. And I, *I* had caused it." For one tiny moment her bottom lip quivered.

"What did they do?" Mark asked softly.

Kim removed his arm from her shoulder. "Listen, this is getting crazy. I mean, I don't want any pity. It was a great learning experience. Really. In one fell swoop, I saw myself for what I was—a useless little street punk. After that, I cleaned up my act."

"What did they do?" Mark persisted.

Her mouth tightened. "They told me to get away or they'd call the police, and when my friends gathered round, they made good on their threat. An officer was patrolling the park nearby and flew over like a shot. He didn't really do anything, just told us to be on our way."

"And did you?"

"Yes. End of story." Kim hauled herself off the threshold. "I had to find out about becoming a nanny at the library."

Mark sat with his arms loosely draped across his knees, staring up at her. Kim was trying to act indifferent, but he knew the incident had hurt. Hurt? It had changed her life. And if she was acting tough, that was only her way of hiding the pain.

She tossed her hair back with a sharp snap of her head. "I've seen enough of this crummy shack. Let's hit the road."

Mark wasn't fooled for a minute.

THROUGHOUT THEIR MEAL that evening, the tiny red light on the phone blinked on and off, telling them there were messages waiting to be played. They'd ordered pizza and laid a fire, then sat on the rented Oriental rug, pretending they couldn't see into the study where the message light continued to blink its malevolent red eye.

Finally Kim tossed her crumpled napkin into the empty pizza box and faced the fact that the weekend was over. They were back in the real world, and none of their problems had gone away. If anything, they'd come home with more, she thought, watching the play of shadow on Mark's handsome sun-bronzed face, over the mouth whose addictive taste she wished she'd never discovered.

She glanced away, burying the pain that momentarily had risen too near the surface. "Ready whenever you are."

Mark got up reluctantly and walked off to his study. By the time he returned, the first message was playing—Suzanne, asking where he was. The second message was also from Suzanne. "For heaven's sake, Mark, what did you think you were doing, walking out in the middle of the day? I came up with every excuse I could to save your hide. And I did save it, I'll have you know. But Father is still ripped, and so am I. Call me as soon as you get in."

Kim flashed Mark an alarmed look. "You walked out?"

He shrugged and tipped back his beer mug.

The next message concerned the newspaper photo, an inevitability Kim had been dreading. Yet, surprisingly, this message left her laughing. It came from a woman whose strident complaints meandered everywhere, from gambling and Kim's outfit, to drugs, acid rain and the price of oil.

"I guess the radio talk-show line was busy." Mark was still chuckling when the next message started.

"Mark? Bob in New York. Give me a call as soon as you can..."

Suddenly, Mark shot to his feet and dashed toward the study.

"I checked out the Registry of Deeds," the message went on, "and have some interesting news regarding the sixteenth." Mark finally reached the machine and hit the Off button, but the message had already played out.

A hot blade seemed to lodge in Kim's midsection. When Mark returned, he looked equally stricken.

"What's that all about?" she asked, barely breathing.

"Nothing. Business."

"For a lawyer, you can't lie worth a damn, Johnson. The sixteenth was the day Miriam was supposed to sign over the papers to the house, but the people buying it backed out. Don't tell me that message is just a coincidence."

Mark gripped the back of his neck. "All right. I didn't want to upset you before we left, and there's still probably a good explanation—"

"What? What?" She flailed her arms.

"I tried calling Miriam last week, but all I got was a recording saying that her number was no longer in service."

Kim turned to the fire and wrapped her arms around her knees. She hadn't thought about Miriam for days. At Breckenridge she'd breathed so blessedly free of her fears and uncertainties. But now a familiar sense of dread crawled up her spine.

"When I couldn't get in touch with her," Mark continued, "I got concerned. So I called an old friend of mine who lives in New York and asked him to check into it."

"Was that him?"

"Yes."

Kim nodded woodenly. "I see. Well, better go find out what he has to say."

She was lying on her back, staring at the shadows flickering across the ceiling, when Mark returned. He sat beside her, very still. The room was silent except for the hiss and pop of the fire.

"In my experience," Kim said in what she thought was a remarkably philosophic tone, "bad news usually comes this way. On tiptoe."

Mark took a deep breath and let it out slowly. "She sold the house, Kim."

"Ah." Kim concentrated with all her might on the dancing shadows, as elusive as mercury.

"She signed the papers on the sixteenth, the day she was supposed to. Nobody backed out of any deal."

For a moment, Kim's throat tightened and she thought she would cry. She sat up quickly and stared into the white heart of the fire. "Then, she lied to me."

"To me, too." Mark sounded hollow. "Do you have any idea why?"

Kim ached too much to talk.

"Kim, please. Don't close up on me now."

But she continued to stare at the fire, wanting to sink into herself until she disappeared. Abruptly Mark sat up on his haunches, gripped her arms and turned her forcibly.

"Look at me, dammit. Maybe withdrawing was the way you coped with disappointment in the past, but you're not going to go through this one alone."

Kim lowered her head and shook it side to side. He didn't have a clue. Disappointment? Good heaven, her insides felt mangled.

As quickly as he'd grabbed her, he let her go. "Huh. Just as I thought. You're really just a selfish little wimp, all wound up in your own problems. Geez, Kim, don't you even care what might've happened to Miriam? Do you dislike her that much? After she raised you and loved you? After she sent you out here to better yourself? What kind of heartless bitch are you, anyway?"

Kim looked up, totally stunned. From out of nowhere, something inside her snapped, and she gave Mark's chest a two-fisted shove that knocked him backward. "Me, a bitch? Me? I don't believe this! Your sister treated me with about as much love as that doorknob is capable of giving. All she ever wanted from me was my paycheck, and then when she found herself sitting on a nice little nest egg, she couldn't push me out the door fast enough. And the only reason her phone is disconnected now is she doesn't want anyone bothering her while she and Theodore are living it up on my father's money, which, granted, isn't much, but it's something, and a fortune to me, and if she had even a shred of decency in her..."

Mark sat up, not in the least upset. Kim's tirade slowed. He looked so pleased with himself he was almost grinning. She grew confused, wary. What was going on here?

All at once, the light dawned. "Damn you, Mark Johnson. You baited me." She raised her hand and slugged him again. Immediately heat blazed in her cheeks. "Oh, Mark, I'm sorry."

"No. Don't be afraid of the anger, Kim. Let it out."

But she couldn't. It was gone, lost in her confusion.

Mark caught up her hand and brought her palm to his lips. Under the heat of his breath her fingers relaxed. He smiled, gently, then gathered her to him. "You've obviously been harboring a great deal of anger toward Miriam, and it's high time we discussed it, don't you think?"

Kim slid her cheek fractionally against his blue chambray shirt. "You smell like wood smoke and beer."

"Don't change the subject. Now what's this all about, Miriam sitting on a nest egg? And who's Theodore?"

Kim moved out of his disconcerting embrace. "I'd really rather not get into this with you, do you mind?"

"Yes, I do. She's my sister. I have a right to know."

Kim groaned. The last thing she wanted to do was play the spoiler with Mark's childhood memories. "It's nothing."

"Are you going to tell me, or shall I call my friend in New York again?"

"Who is this friend, anyway? A cop?"

"A private investigator, and he's *very* good."

Kim slumped in defeat. "All right. But don't say you weren't warned." She paused to pull in a breath. "Miriam inherited everything my father left."

Mark looked at her dubiously. "But surely he provided for you in his will, too."

"My father died intestate."

"I see. But even without a will, you would've inherited—"

"Nothing."

"Nothing?"

"That's right. After my father and Miriam were married, they had the deed on our house changed from his name to theirs. Tenancy by the entirety, survivor takes all."

"But that was originally your grandmother's house."

Kim felt a familiar cold tide of resentment wash through her, but all she said was, "Ah, well, it was a dump, anyway. Who cares?"

Mark eyed her sharply. "How about an insurance policy?"

Kim shook her head. "Miriam was the sole beneficiary. My dad put that in her name, too."

"How much are we talking here?"

"In insurance? Fifteen thousand dollars."

"And the house?"

"Miriam was asking ninety thousand."

Mark sat quietly, running his knuckles over his chin. "If Miriam's name had stayed off those documents, your father's estate would've had to be probated, and you would've inherited a large portion. You realize that, don't you?"

Kim nodded.

"Did Miriam get anything else?"

"Besides the household furnishings? Sure, a thirty-thousand-dollar lump-sum settlement from my father's pension plan."

"Ouch."

"Hey, she was his wife. She has every right to it."

Mark studied her skeptically. "Did you ever think of fighting the settlement?"

Kim stared at the fire, afraid that guilt was written on her face. "No. Why would I do that?" She pulled at a curl and twirled it round a finger.

Mark breathed out a laugh. "You didn't get very far, I take it?"

Her hair-twirling stopped. When had Mark learned to read her so well? "No. But I don't care, really. I'm ashamed of having done it, especially since Miriam came up with this plan to move at almost the same time. It was the most generous, exciting invitation. She said we'd start a new life here together, and she'd help me, you know, with school and all." Kim ducked her head, garbling her last words.

"And you believed her?"

Kim's breath burned in her throat. "I wanted to, but secretly I had my doubts. It's why... it's why I felt compelled to find a job right away, to start saving money. I'm not used to people coming through on their promises."

"I wonder why," Mark said sardonically. "With a mother who took off when you were a baby, and a father who was never sober, and a grandmother—"

"Hey! My grandmother was wonderful."

"Thank God. You needed somebody. But she did, well, die on you."

"Yes, I suppose she did," Kim agreed sadly.

"So who's this Theodore person?"

"Theodore? Uh, just a friend."

"Kimberly!"

She peeked up into his stern face and knew he'd press until she talked. "He's your sister's new boyfriend."

"New . . . Already?"

Kim nodded. "I figure you'll get to meet Theo about a week after Miriam arrives."

Mark looked away quickly.

"What's the matter?" A sudden wariness prickled her scalp.

"Kim, my friend in New York... Bob went round to your old house, pretending to be doing a survey on cable TV service. The guy's pretty imaginative. . . ."

"And did he see Miriam?"

"Yes, she was there, but it was evident that she was about to move. A U-Haul was parked at the curb and packing crates were stacked to the rafters. That was Friday, the day we left for Breckenridge."

Kim didn't like the guardedness of Mark's voice. "So?"

"Bob stopped by again today."

"And?"

"And the place was empty."

Kim's pulse hammered crazily although outwardly she remained impassive. "Ah. So I guess the only thing we can do is wait. How long do you think it'll take her to get here?"

Mark trailed the back of his hand down her cheek. "What I'm trying to say is, I don't think we should wait. When Bob was doing his phony survey, Miriam tripped up. She told him she didn't need cable TV because she was moving. But not to Colorado, Kim." Mark paused, his expression darkening. "She said she was going down South."

CHAPTER NINE

"DOWN SOUTH?" Kim's vision swam.

"That's what Bob said."

In a haze of emotion, Kim got to her feet and stumbled to a window. *So, Miriam's abandoned me, too,* she thought, a choking sensation rising in her throat. *She's packed up and headed for a new life, forgetting I even exist.*

But even as Kim gazed out the dark window, Miriam's actions took on a new clarity. *Damn her!* Miriam had shipped her here purposely to get rid of her. *That* was her secret agenda. She'd never intended to move out here herself, and she'd certainly never intended to help with Kim's training. She wanted to keep every penny of her windfall and had gone to extraordinary measures to do so. As for all that stuff about wanting to forge new family bonds...

Kim laughed miserably as she looked over at Mark. He was still sitting by the fire but had become pensive, self-absorbed. He'd been as big a fool as she. Miriam had used him as a dumping ground, and he hadn't even known it.

Did he know it now? Is that why he was so quiet? A tide of guilt flooded Kim's heart. She'd brought such mayhem to his life, and now this, this terrible disillusionment. And why? There wasn't a single good reason. This move to Colorado was nothing but a misbegotten detour in the course of her life. A profound sadness settled in her heart. It was clearly time to set things right.

"Mark?"

Her voice seemed to startle him. "Yes, kitten?"

The endearment nearly did her in. "Mark, I . . . I'm sorry I've put you out all these weeks. It seems my coming here was all quite unnecessary, wasn't it? I wish I had the means to repay you, but the only thing I can do is apologize and—" she gulped "—be out of here as soon as possible."

Mark blinked several times. "What are you talking about?"

Her right hand slid up to her hair and began its habitual twirling. "Well, your sister was the only reason you put me up, and now that we know she's not coming . . ."

Mark hauled himself off the floor and in a flash crossed the distance that separated them. "Don't be absurd. Where would you go? You have no other family, and your financial situation isn't exactly the greatest."

"I have enough money to get back to New York, by bus if need be."

He gripped her arms, his eyes trained hard on hers. "And then what? You'd be in a worse fix than you're in now."

"I can stay with a friend for a while," she offered, but only halfheartedly. Charlotte's parents' home was small.

"For how long? New York rents are exorbitant, and you'd still have your training to pay for."

Mark was right, and suddenly Kim wondered why she was arguing. The last thing she wanted to do was leave, but not for the reasons he'd given. Kim couldn't bear leaving *him*. Mark had become the center of her existence, and even if he didn't love her the way she loved him, being near was better than being two thousand miles away.

She nodded. "Okay. You're right."

His hold on her arms relaxed. "Good." He paced a few steps, forward, back, one hand pressed to the nape of his neck. "I'm not sure what Miriam is up to, Kim, but more than likely she'll call soon to explain. She usually does. And who knows? She might've already made provisions for you, or . . . or she might want you to join her wherever she is down South."

"You don't really believe that, do you?" As soon as she'd said it she was sorry.

Mark paused, his expression drooping. "I don't know, I don't know." He resumed his pacing. "In the meantime, I don't want you worrying about a roof over your head or a job or school. I don't have any answers tonight, but we'll find them. We will, I promise. You're not in this alone."

Kim swallowed hard. She so wanted to believe him, but did she dare? Mark didn't owe her anything. Their ties didn't exactly run deep or long. "Thank you," she said flatly.

"No problem. Now, why don't you go turn in. It's been a long day and if you don't mind, I'd like to sit here by myself awhile."

KIM GOT HOME late the next afternoon. She parked the Cherokee in the driveway, surprised to see the BMW already there. "Mark?" she called, coming in the front door.

"In here."

Mark was sitting in the living room reading the newspaper. His hair fell in an untidy shock over his brow and his tie drooped at half-mast. Kim paused in the doorway, struck by how deeply the sight of him always affected her.

"Where've you been?" He peered at her over his reading glasses.

"Out looking for a job."

"Really? Come here." He patted the couch beside him.

The news that Miriam had sold the house and skipped off had kept Kim awake nearly the whole night. She'd arisen depressed and moped about her room all morning, feeling lost and rootless. Although she and Miriam had never been close, Miriam was the last vestige of family she had, and now even she was gone.

But after writing in her journal, Kim had felt immeasurably better. Putting her feelings into words always clarified them for her and gave her an orderly perspective. She'd showered, dressed and with new determination got on with her life. Miriam might be gone, but so was the uncertainty Kim had lived with all the months since her father's death, waiting on Miriam's dubious promises. Now she knew exactly where she stood, what lay ahead, what needed to be done.

Besides, she wasn't really alone. Mark had offered to help, and while she knew his help could only be temporary, it would be sufficient to get her on her feet. She shouldn't have doubted him last evening. Mark was a man of his word, and since her arrival, his actions had revealed nothing but caring. She'd closed this morning's entry with the optimistic line "God's in his heaven. All's right with the world."

"Come sit," Mark repeated, removing his glasses.

Kim nudged off her shoes and sat, folding her legs under her. "How was your day? Any repercussions after walking out last Friday?"

He laughed. "Sure were. The partners were ripping."

"Mark! How can you laugh about such a thing?"

He folded the paper and tossed it onto the coffee table. "Because they finally got to see Zambroski in action, and apparently it wasn't a pretty sight. So, what's this about looking for a job?" He rested his arm along the back of the sofa so that it skimmed her shoulders. His jaw was shadowed by a day's growth of beard, lending the sensuous curve of his mouth an added appeal.

In the tumult of the latest events, Kim had temporarily forgotten how strong the physical pull between them was. At Breckenridge they'd vowed to control it, and for a short time other concerns had done the job for them. But apparently their attraction wasn't a rational obedient entity, and right now a simple resting of an arm along a sofa was fraught with all the danger of a full-blown seduction.

"I got a job," she said, sitting forward.

"You did?" Mark frowned. "Where?"

"Another restaurant, but don't worry, this one's straight. I did a lot of thinking this morning, and I've decided to go ahead with my plan to train for certification. Here in Colorado. But I have a favor to ask first."

Mark took a strand of her hair and coiled it round his finger. "What's that?"

For a moment, her mind went blank as she lost herself in his deep blue eyes. "I was wondering if we could agree on some sort of equitable living arrangement so I don't have to move out on my own just yet. Housekeeping in exchange for room and board maybe. Just until I've saved enough to cover tuition and living expenses during training."

"Kim, I'll gladly lend you the money."

"No. I'll do this on my own."

"That's what I thought you'd say. That's why..." Mark uncoiled her hair and trailed his finger along her jawline.

"Why what?"

"I found you a job, too," he finished.

"You what?"

"I thought about your predicament and came to the conclusion that you're wasting your time working in restaurants and offices. Those jobs have nothing to do with the nanny business. What you've got to do is get on with it, forget dreaming about the future. The future is now, kitten."

Kim felt a tremor in the pit of her stomach. "What did you do?"

He smiled, enthusiasm glittering in his eyes. "While I was at the office today, I took the liberty of calling around, and I found you a post."

"A post? You mean...?"

"Yes, as a nanny. The couple want to interview you, of course, but from the sales pitch I gave them, I'd say that's going to be a cakewalk."

"Where did you find these people?"

"They're friends of mine. Paul and Chrissie Mitchell. They have two children, a boy and a girl." He stopped, his eyes narrowing. "What's the matter? You don't look too thrilled."

Kim raised her trembling hand and placed it over his lips. "No. Just stunned. One minute I was here, the next on a roller coaster. Wait. I'll catch up."

Mark sighed, a small vee etched between his eyes. "I didn't mean to rush you, but once I get a notion..."

"But what'll I do about training?"

"If the certificate really means that much..."

"It does."

"Then go for it. Save the money you earn at the Mitchells' and do it. I fully realize this isn't Manhattan and you have an image of yourself pushing a stroller down Fifth Avenue, and I'm not saying you should give up that dream, but this is a better stepping stone than slinging dishes in some lousy restaurant. It's hands-on experience, and even more important, it'll be a valuable reference. If you decide you still want to head back to New York, the Mitchells have connections."

Kim dragged her hands down her face, laughing nervously. "This is scary. You know, be careful what you wish for...?"

"Don't worry. You'll do fine." He moved toward her again, his hand drifting to her back. Kim closed her eyes, feeling his warmth and caring flow into her. How wonderful it would be if only Mark would let this closeness follow its natural course, as it had over the weekend.

"So," she said, primly folding her hands in her lap, "give me the details."

He lowered his arm. "Details. Well, I think you'll get a kick out of the Mitchells' house. It's one of the grander homes in the city. They have so much room, you'll have an entire suite to yourself. Paul's great-grandfather owned an ore refinery during—"

Kim clamped a hand on Mark's knee. "Stop. Back up." Panic was rising again. "I'll be living *with* them?"

"Of course. Isn't that a given?"

"Not necessarily. Some nannies only come in days."

"Well, Chrissie made it clear she wants live-in help."

Kim sat very still, letting the fact sink in. "Oh, Mark."

"I know." His voice was low and dark. "But being out on your own was always your objective, anyway. Right?"

Of course it was. So why was the thought of moving out suddenly filling her with dread? She should be happy, instead of thinking how much she'd miss Mark. She should be lavishing him with gratitude instead of fighting off tears.

"You'll only be four blocks away, kitten. If you ever need anything, I'll be right here."

Kim wanted to believe him. Lord, it would be heaven to have someone in her life as dependable as Mark appeared. But she'd had too many bad experiences. She knew this moment was really the beginning of the end. People came into your life and they drifted out. It was as natural as waves lapping on a beach. Nobody ever really stayed, not even the ones who loved you, and Mark had more reasons than most for wanting to sever the ties.

"Well, thank you," she answered shakily. "Thanks for everything—your hospitality, the new clothes, the ski trip..."

Mark turned, surprised by the catch in her voice. He cupped her face in both hands, his steady blue eyes reaching into her, deep, deeper with every scintillating second. "Thanks for letting me come along for the ride."

Kim prided herself on being tough in painful situations, but there was a lump in her throat as big as a baseball.

She lifted her hands to his face, cradling it in the same manner he was holding hers. Dear Lord, she was so deeply in love with this man. She hadn't meant it to happen, and she was sure he'd be appalled if he knew. But somehow, somewhere, she'd tripped up and fallen, totally.

"Mark?" Her voice was filled with fear and confusion and so unsteady she wasn't sure she even made a sound.

But he heard, and his lips dipped to hers in answer. The kiss was tender, sweet, just what she needed at this fragile moment in her life.

"This is a very bad situation. You know that, don't you?" she whispered, her lips brushing his.

"The worst," he whispered back.

"We said we weren't going to do this anymore."

"I know."

But a moment later they were lost in a kiss deeper and more powerful than anything Kim had ever imagined possible. And it was just what she needed at *that* moment.

She clung to him with a desperation that rose from a lifetime of being unloved, and from there a fire soon leapt, one that had nothing to do with her past or with her future. Her ardor tipped them over onto the cushions of the couch, and when she felt crushed beneath his warm heavy weight, she kissed him deeper still. She heard him moan as her mouth opened to meet his hot exploration.

"Kim, you're driving me crazy," he panted, coming up for air.

Her ego soared. What power, to move a man as virile as Mark, to affect him so easily. She smiled as she gazed into his desire-glazed eyes.

"Aw, hell, don't do that."

"Do what?"

"Smile. I can't...uh..." A moment later he was kissing her again, hard, thoroughly. "Can't resist your smile," he finished in a rush.

They tumbled off the couch onto the floor. She was sure Mark hit his elbow on the coffee table, yet he never broke the seal of their kiss.

She landed fully on top of him, her skirt askew, hair waterfalling around his face. "Just what you need, a cracked elbow."

He grinned against her lips. "That's not the part of me I'm concerned about at the moment."

Kim's already hot cheeks grew fevered.

"Sorry. I didn't mean to embarrass you." He combed back her hair, twisting strands between his fingers.

Kim slid to the floor and lay beside him, one arm resting at his waist. "I'm the one who should apologize. I'm just not—" she stared at the ceiling "—very experienced at this sort of thing."

Mark braced himself up on one elbow, eyeing her hawkishly. "Just how not-very-experienced are we talking here?"

"Not...not experienced at all." Kim decided if she didn't die of embarrassment there and then, she never would. She'd grown up with girls who'd started experimenting with sex at fourteen, girls who'd been pregnant at sixteen, become prostitutes at eighteen. And here she was, twenty-two and still a rank novice.

Mark sat up, leaning against the couch they'd tumbled off in their passion. "And that embarrasses you?"

"Well, yes. I've seen the women you take out. I can imagine what you're used to."

Mark grinned. "Apparently not." His fingertips lightly stroked one stockinged leg. "Kitten, on a scale of one to ten, where ten's the very hottest date I've ever had, you're somewhere around a ninety-two."

Kim ducked her head, wanting to laugh with joy.

"And that's just on the basis of how you kiss. I can't imagine what making love..." Mark's eyes took on a hard brilliance as they drove into hers.

Kim's senses reeled. She leaned toward him, drawn by his whispery voice, by the fire in his eyes, leaned until their lips were only a breath apart. With the unfinished sentence sizzling between them, they joined in a kiss that made her feel she was exploding from the outside in.

When Mark finally pulled away, Kim was boneless. Slowly she opened her eyes and smiled. But Mark wasn't smiling back. He looked upset.

"Oh, Kim. Now do you see why we can't stay under the same roof any longer?" Although his voice was thick with lingering passion, it still conveyed an anger and frustration that startled her. He got to his feet and walked away.

Left sitting on the floor, Kim felt cold and abandoned. "N-no, I don't see."

Mark raked back his disheveled hair with two hands. His eyes looked haunted. "Kim, this . . . this relationship we're developing isn't right. I'm supposed to be helping you, not taking advantage."

"I fail to see how you're taking advantage if I—"

"That's just it. You fail to see."

"See what?" Her voice cracked.

Mark stepped behind a club chair, using its back to brace his hands. "That you're terribly vulnerable at this point in your life. You're young and alone, stranded in a strange city without any means of support. You've been knocked around by everyone who's ever meant anything to you, and now here I am, here I am, probably filling every emotional need you've ever had—father, mother, friend, lover . . ."

Kim gasped. "That's not true!"

"Isn't it? I'm afraid you may be all mixed up right now and unable to see it. Most people in your situation would be. And I don't want to mix you up any more than you already are. I don't want the responsibility or the guilt."

Kim stared at him incredulously. "I may be mixed up but not half as much as you are, Mark. At least I know physical attraction when I see it."

"Of course, there's that, too. You're a very desirable woman, Kim. Anybody would be attracted to you, given this living arrangement. That's what I'm trying to tell you."

For a moment Kim only heard the words "desirable woman," but then she realized what Mark was saying. Even as he was flattering her, he was saying he didn't take his attraction to her seriously. It was nothing more than an automatic male response. She still fell short of the mark. Too young. Too unsophisticated. Too everything. And worst of all he was couching his rejection of her in altruistic excuses.

"Of course. You're right," she said coolly, swallowing her heartache. When would she ever learn? He'd done this to her at Breckenridge, yet she'd let herself forget the pain and come back for more. Only, each time it got worse.

"Sure I'm right. We need to put some distance between us, Kim."

The ache inside her grew. No matter what he said about not wanting to hurt her while she was vulnerable, the truth was he didn't want her in his life any more than anyone else had.

"Let's grab a bite to eat," she said. "After supper I'll call the Mitchells and arrange an interview." It was clearly time to leave.

TWO NIGHTS LATER Mark slipped Kim's high-school graduation picture into a frame and set it on his desk. He'd had to wrestle it from her. She'd said she didn't want anyone seeing what a "dork" she'd been at seventeen. A dork.

Mark braced his chin on his hand and smiled through a bittersweet pang. She looked younger, her hair was shorter, but even at seventeen, she'd been a stunner.

He leaned back in his leather chair, hands linked atop his head, and listened to the silence of his house. She'd moved out this morning while he'd been at the office. He was glad he'd been gone.

Her leaving was all for the best, he reminded himself for at least the tenth time that evening. She really was too vulnerable at this point in her life, and he didn't want to add to her emotional muddle. And he would add to it, too, if she stayed. The physical draw between them was far too strong. Mark closed his eyes. At times he couldn't believe how strong. In her presence he couldn't think straight, couldn't do anything except burn.

And it wasn't right. She'd end up expecting more from him than he could give.

Mark stood up and aimlessly roamed his new study. If he was perfectly honest, there was one other reason he'd initiated this separation, a reason he'd refused to examine until now. It involved his feelings toward Miriam and the way they were changing.

He'd hoped to keep Miriam separate from Kim. He'd wanted to be able to like them both. But the more he'd gotten to know Kim, the harder it had been to keep Miriam in a neat compartment.

He didn't want to dislike his sister. She was his only living relative. They shared the same genes, shared the same memories, of the farm, of their parents, of prairie dust and bland meals—and sitting under stars and dreaming dreams.

But, dammit, this last stunt had been too much. Not only was it a hell of a thing to do to Kim, but Miriam had used *him* to do it. She'd betrayed the love and trust that had connected them all these years. Until now he'd made excuses for her behavior toward others, saying life had dealt her a bad hand and she was only trying to survive as best she could, but the excuses didn't wash anymore. She'd used him, she'd lied, as if he was just *anybody*.

Mark returned to his chair, picked up the photograph taken at his college graduation and felt a constriction in his chest. Such a cruel lie, too, saying she was moving here because she wanted to be closer to him. Now he understood Kim's plight. He'd been deserted as soundly as she.

He put down the picture, feeling a headache coming on. He knew it was unfair to blame Kim for the way his perception of his sister had changed, and he wasn't really *blaming* her. But if Kim hadn't come out here, that perception would still be untarnished.

And therein lay the subtler reason he'd found Kim this nanny job. She was the solid reminder of Miriam's deceit, and if the reminder was out of sight, perhaps his awareness of the deceit would vanish, also. Mark wasn't sure it was possible to pull the wool back over one's own eyes, but that was exactly what he aimed to do.

Right after he found some aspirin for this headache. Before he could push himself out of his chair, however, the phone rang.

"Yes?"

"Hello, my friend."

"Bob? Hey, how's it going?"

Tonight Bob Cooper was full of news. Yesterday he'd visited the couple who'd bought Miriam's house and discovered she'd left behind several shipping cartons. Not knowing what they were, the new occupants had opened them.

"It didn't take a rocket scientist to figure out the stuff belonged to the girl," Bob said.

Mark took out his frustration on the clicker of a ballpoint pen.

"I have everything here at my place now. They were glad to be rid of it. Should I ship it to you?"

"Mmm, please. I'm sure Kim'll be tickled to receive it."

"Yup. There's all sorts of stuff here. Clothes, junk jewelry, old dolls, *diaries.*"

Mark was sure the term "pregnant pause" had been invented for the silence that followed. "Okay, I'll bite," he finally said. "What did you find in the diaries?" The pen was clicking at an unholy rate now.

"The kid's mother ran off when she was three."

"Old news."

"Okay. How about, did you know she's been working since the age of eleven?"

The clicking stopped. "Uh, no."

"And when she was twelve she was held up at knifepoint for a measly eight bucks in paper-route money?"

Mark threw the pen and let fly a string of curses. "Where the hell was her father during all this, that good-for-nothing drunk."

"Usually at a bar called Sandy's. Hey, how does this grab you? The kid scored 640 on the verbal part of her SATs."

Mark gazed at Kim's photograph in mounting anger, wondering why nobody had bothered to cultivate her potential.

"Evidently she wanted to go on to school," Bob continued, "but, I'm gonna be honest with you, my friend, your sister was a first-rate witch. Not that the kid whined about it or anything, but I can read between the lines. Seems your sister thought education was a waste of time. She kept the kid working and bled her dry."

Mark got to his feet and paced as far as the cord would reach. "Okay, okay, just mail the stuff on." He'd heard enough for one night.

"Sure. Oh, one more thing. Your sister's in Florida. Want her address?"

"Yes!" Mark retrieved his pen from the floor and scribbled the address. "How'd you find her?"

"Easy. Her U-Haul bill. By the way, if you happen to call her and a man answers, that's just her new husband."

Mark closed his eyes. No, he shouldn't be angry. Miriam did stuff like this all the time. He was used to it.

But he *was* angry. Dammit, he was very angry. The woman hadn't the slightest regard for anyone but herself.

He slumped into his leather chair and propped his forehead against his hand. He didn't want to think about Miriam anymore.

Or Kim. He'd done more for that gorgeous little thorn in his side than he'd ever intended. He'd become involved, set her on a course of independence, and she wasn't his responsibility anymore. She wasn't.

"Listen, Bob. I have one more job for you. Kim's natural mother—do you think you can track her down? I've been thinking, with Kim alone now, maybe her mother would like to get to know her, maybe even help her out."

"Whew! That's a long shot."

"I don't care how much time it takes or how much money."

"All right. I'll try."

Mark hung up the phone, telling himself his conscience was now clear. Tracking down Kim's mother was above and beyond anyone's definition of responsibility.

After a moment's contemplation, he dialed Suzanne's number and invited her to dinner the following evening. While Kim had been living here, he and Suzanne had barely seen each other, except at the office. Suzanne accepted.

With that part of his life back on track, Mark put on his glasses and opened his briefcase. It was time to get the rest of his affairs on track, too.

But five minutes later, instead of working, Mark was staring at Kim's photograph and listening to the silence of his house.

CHAPTER TEN

THE MITCHELLS WERE a couple in their midthirties. Paul owned a brokerage firm, and Chrissie stayed home because she adored being a housewife.

"I love to cook," the tiny blonde explained to Kim, waltzing her through a tour of the kitchen. "But only occasionally." And so she had a cook "to back her up." Chrissie loved gardening, too—but not all the time—and so there was a gardener. A cleaning woman came in for similar reasons, and now there was Kim to help with the children.

As far as Kim could see, Chrissie didn't do much of anything thoroughly, but instead flitted through her day as unfocused as a bat at noon. But being unfocused wasn't the worst fault Kim had ever encountered in a person, and Chrissie did like to talk and laugh. No one could ever accuse her of being stuck-up. After being there a week, Kim could honestly say she liked the woman.

And she loved the children, handfuls though they were. Baby Bethany had an aversion to napping, even though she was only thirteen months old. Hence, for half the day she was a delightful toddler, but for the next half, a cranky monster. And four-year-old Jason was into playing superheroes, with the full accompaniment of expensive outfits, vehicles guaranteed to reach warp-speed in ten seconds and enough playground equipment to train a regular army battalion.

Yet, they were still children, babies really, and Kim embraced them with a patience and an understanding that Chrissie called miraculous.

If the children had any problem, Kim decided, it was that they seemed overstimulated. Too many people bustling about their house, too many toys, too ebullient a mother. They needed quiet play, needed someone to snuggle with over a Peter Rabbit story. They needed to creep about the backyard observing ants and worms and other mysterious creatures peeping out to enjoy the spring sunshine. They needed warm milk at night instead of soda, perhaps a lullaby or a comforting massage...

By the end of the first week, Bethany took her first afternoon nap in months, and by the end of the second, Jason was more engrossed in *building* cardboard forts for his action figures to storm than in the actual storming itself. Kim couldn't have been more pleased. The children were genuinely lovable. She got along well with their parents. She had three comfortable rooms all to herself, Wednesdays and Sundays free and a very handsome salary. It was everything she'd ever hoped to achieve, and she didn't even have her certification yet.

Then why wasn't she happy? she wondered, as the third week came to a close.

"THIS MAKES NO SENSE whatsoever," Kim complained as the Mitchell's Mercedes purred to a stop at a local nightspot called the Golden Bee. "Hiring a baby-sitter to take out the nanny is crazy."

"Except when it's her birthday," Paul replied. "Besides, you haven't been anywhere since you started working for us. All work and no play..."

"...makes the nanny a well-dressed lady," Kim finished, tugging at the sleeve of her jacket, part of a pantsuit she'd recently bought in her determination to replace her old wardrobe.

She could already hear music, a boisterous piano and people singing "Roll out the Barrel."

"What sort of place is this, anyway?"

Chrissie giggled. "If you can't have fun here, Kim, I'm afraid you're a lost cause."

The pub was crowded, and they had to wait in the lobby for a table, listening enviously to the revelry inside. Sometime during that wait, Kim was stunned to discover that Mark and Suzanne had joined them. She'd been so engrossed in the music she hadn't seen them come in.

Slowly she rose from her chair, unable to sort her rioting emotions. Mark had visited her only twice since she'd moved, and each visit had been short and businesslike. On one of those occasions he'd informed her that Miriam had remarried. On the next, he'd brought her the boxes she'd left behind in Brooklyn. Each time, she'd gotten the impression he was trying to put more distance between them. His brusqueness had hurt.

"How are you, Kimberly?"

Kimberly. More distance.

"I'm fine," she replied with feigned indifference. "Hello, Suzanne."

Suzanne clung to Mark's arm, smiling with a smugness that seemed to say "I won, I won." Perhaps she had, Kim thought despondently. While Kim had been living with Mark, she hadn't sensed anything more serious between him and Suzanne than a casual dating relationship, but perhaps she'd been wrong. Perhaps something had blossomed after she'd moved out. After all, that was the direction his life had been heading when she'd arrived.

"We asked Mark to join us, since his birthday is next Tuesday," Paul explained. "We thought we'd make this a doubleheader."

"Well, how nice." Kim smiled genially even as she wondered how she'd make it through the evening. Her emotions were too near the surface, threatening to expose her for the lovesick fool she was.

Just then, the doorman signaled that their table was ready. They went in and were seated. Paul and Chrissie. Mark and Suzanne. And Kim.

Sighing into her chair, she resigned herself to her perennial singleness. It was her birthday, and alone though she was, she ought to try to have a good time. Forget the fact that she felt miserable. Forget that the person she most wanted to see tonight was here with somebody else. The Mitchells had been thoughtful enough to invite her out; she ought to return that thoughtfulness by appearing happy.

Fortunately Paul and Chrissie couldn't have chosen a better spot. The atmosphere at the Golden Bee was a cross between an Irish pub, a medieval tavern and an Old West dance hall, and before long, Kim was singing and waving her mug of ale just as merrily as everyone else.

But her gaiety was forced. At best, she was enduring the evening. At worst, she occasionally felt ill. And the cause of her distress was always Mark. He ignored her conversation, evaded her eyes and bestowed all his attention on Suzanne. Evidently Mark had been able to put her out of his life with ease and wasn't looking back.

Yet twice she caught him watching her. He glanced away quickly but not before she noticed the curiously wistful expression in his eyes. During those moments she wondered what he was thinking. Was he remembering Breckenridge and the fun they'd been able to have there because they'd been free of constraints? Did he miss that freedom? That honesty of emotion? Did he miss *her?*

But of course the thought was absurd. If anything, he had reason to rejoice. He *was* free—now. Free to go about his life as he had before she'd interrupted it.

The evening wore on. They ate a light supper. They sang. They laughed at the people who ordered their ale in yard-long beakers and had such difficulty drinking. And finally a waiter surprised them with a cake, topped with two candles, and the piano player led everyone in singing "Happy Birthday." Kim smiled and rolled her eyes, pleasing her hosts with her mock-embarrassment.

But her will to be merry was quickly running out of steam. Her throat was tightening and the burning in her eyes wouldn't clear. She didn't understand her unhappiness in the midst of all this singing and celebration. She had so much to be grateful for.

Cautiously she lifted her eyes and let them meet Mark's. Their serious blue-violet depths glinted with candlelight, reminding her of another candlelit moment in their lives, that seemingly perfect night at Breckenridge exactly three weeks ago. And as she stared, even as the candles between them burned and the room rocked in celebration, it hit her. Kim knew precisely why she was so unhappy, with her job, with her life. The insight struck like a thunderbolt.

"Okay, you two," Chrissie said as the clapping faded. "Make a wish and blow out your candles."

From opposite sides of the table, Mark and Kim leaned in, thoughtful, their eyes locked. The irony of the situation was almost too much to bear. She knew what she wanted above all else, but with equal certainty, she knew she'd never get it.

The smoke was still spiraling from the candles when she excused herself. She was afraid she couldn't hold back the tears much longer.

"Kimberly?"

Halfway to the women's room, she stopped, her shoulders tensed.

"Kim, is something wrong?"

Slowly she turned, dredging up one more valiant smile. "No. What could possibly be wrong?"

Mark placed his fists on his hips and studied her. "Well, you sure as hell don't look happy."

"So, what's it to you?" She sounded peevish, instead of cavalier, as she'd intended.

Mark's eyes narrowed. "Come here." He took her arm and pulled her into the entryway.

"Hey! What are you doing?" she protested.

"Trying to find a place where we can talk. This is better." He turned her so that her back was to a wall, then braced his hands on either side of her head. The gesture created an intimacy she hadn't anticipated, especially after suffering a night of his indifference.

"Now, what's wrong?"

Everything, she thought, feeling the heat of his body all along the length of her own. "Nothing," she replied. "Look, Mark, we've gone our separate ways. There's no need for you to get involved anymore." She tried to break free, but he held her fast.

"I'm not getting involved. I just want to know what's wrong. Don't you like working for the Mitchells?"

His astuteness disarmed her. "I like it just fine. Everything's perfect." Kim wished he'd stop staring at her.

"If you're unhappy, I wish you'd tell me. I'm the one who got you the job. I feel responsible."

Kim was about to protest once again, but suddenly all the fight went out of her. What was the use? Mark seemed able to read her mind, anyway. "I'll be damned if I can understand it." She sagged against the wall in defeat. "Being a nanny is what I've wanted since I was fifteen." She paused. "No, I *do* understand. It hit me at the table just now, but I guess I don't want to face the reality."

"Which is?"

Kim pulled in a deep breath. "I'm not fifteen anymore. When I was fifteen, those girls pushing baby carriages on Fifth Avenue looked like princesses to me. My experiences were so limited back then. But now it's not what I thought. It's not ... enough."

"Ah." He continued to stare at her in his unsettlingly direct manner.

She had to give him credit. It couldn't be easy to keep looking at someone who was admitting she'd finally reached her goal only to find herself still unhappy. After all, who wanted to connect with a loser?

"So, you've outgrown a dream that fit when you were fifteen. What's wrong with that?" The corner of his mouth turned upward.

"What's wrong? Mark, even I can't stand myself. I come off as a dissatisfied brat who doesn't appreciate the good fortune she's received."

"No. You come off as someone who's finally done the sensible thing and given the job a try to see if she really likes it. An internship, if you will."

Kim studied his handsome features. Mark was amazing. He'd cut her from his life yet still managed to show caring. "But, Mark, I haven't a clue what I'm supposed to do now. My whole world has collapsed."

"No, it hasn't." Grinning, he propped his elbow on the wall and rested his head against his palm. Though he'd released her from the brackets of his arms, Kim still felt very much surrounded by him. "Maybe your world's just opening out, Kim."

She eyed him narrowly. "What do you mean?"

"Well, have you ever considered channeling your interest in child care into a college degree?"

Kim reared back and bumped her head. "No!"

"Maybe you should. Of course, you might be bored much of the time. You've done so much reading already."

"Mark, get serious."

"Kitten, if I got any more serious, you'd have to put me in a coffin."

Kim felt a weakening in her knees. She hadn't expected to be called "kitten" just then. The endearment wrapped them in a warmth that had been missing all evening. "But I've never... What would I do with a college degree?"

"I don't know. Open a nursery school. Become a teacher, a child psychologist, a pediatrician, whatever you find most interesting."

For a moment, Kim's imagination soared, but then she fell back to reality. There was no way she could afford college. Besides, she was already the age of most graduates.

"No. Forget it. I'm fine where I am. Really. I mean it." And she did. She didn't care what she worked at anymore, because while the birthday candles had been flickering between them, she'd discovered something else about herself. She'd realized that when she was fifteen, she'd envied those young nannies primarily because she'd seen them as integral to the families they lived with. She'd seen them as *belonging*. And all those years when she'd dreamed of becoming a nanny herself, all she'd really been doing was hoping to find a place where she belonged, too.

But that wasn't the way it was. As warm as the Mitchells were, she was still just an employee. There was no mistaking who the family was in their house.

Under different circumstances, Kim thought she could've accepted that reality with more grace, but living with Mark, and loving him, had changed her outlook. Now she realized that the family she was seeking was her own, a family she longed to create with Mark. This was what lay at her center. Without Mark, nothing else mattered.

She noticed a frown darkening his handsome face. "Is anything else bothering you?" he asked, leaning even closer. She could practically count his eyelashes. For a moment her head swam, as the desire to kiss him raced through her.

"Uh, no," she said quickly.

He sighed and stepped back from the wall. "You never could lie worth a damn, Wade." He smiled roguishly. "But I'll let it go for now. In the meantime, give that college idea some thought. We have a branch of the state university right here in Colorado Springs, and I'm a pro at filling out those hideous financial-aid forms. I know it's late in the year to be applying, but I'm sure if you went for an interview—''

"Thank you, Mark." Kim placed both palms on his chest to stem the flow of his enthusiasm. "But I'll stay where I am. I'm content."

His mouth tightened, then he nodded in grudging acceptance.

"Before we return to the table..." He lifted his hand and, light as a whisper, ran a finger along her jaw. She shivered, cursing his power to move her. Didn't he know how deeply these flirtations with intimacy hurt?

"I want to wish you a happy twenty-third birthday, kitten."

Her fingers, still resting on his chest, dug into the thick cables of his sweater. Again she feared she might lean forward and press her lips to his. "And a happy thirty-third to you."

"I wish I'd brought you a present."

"No need. You've already given me one."

He frowned. "When?"

"Just now. When you suggested I consider college. You can't imagine what you did for my ego. No one's ever had such high regard for me before. And you said it so naturally, too, as if you just assume I have the capability to get a degree and become anything I please."

"Oh, Kim..." His voice was thick with sadness and frustration.

"Mark?"

Kim jumped at the sound of Suzanne's voice. Mark turned, also, and the closeness that had enveloped them shattered.

"What are you two doing out here?" Neither of them said a word. Suzanne's delicate features hardened. "Your cake is waiting to be cut."

Kim cringed as she envisioned the picture she and Mark presented. Once again she'd landed him in a sticky situation, and Suzanne had every right to be angry.

"Coming, Suzanne. Kim and I were just discussing a private family matter."

Kim watched Mark walk away from her and take Suzanne by the arm.

"Coming, Kim?" he asked almost coolly.

Kim's heart splintered. It seemed she'd never learn that what she took for warmth and caring was nothing more than illusion.

MARK PLACED a frozen dinner in the microwave and set the timer. Then, coffee mug in hand, he sat at the kitchen table and sorted through the day's mail. When he saw Kim's handwriting, his breathing stopped. Today was his birthday, his real birthday, and she'd remembered.

He slit open the envelope and pulled out the card. A child's card. Bugs Bunny. He smiled a smile full of loneliness and regret as an image of the little nightshirt she used to wear flashed across his mind.

Others had remembered his birthday, too, of course. His secretary had brought a cake into work, and Geoff Collins had taken him to lunch. Then Suzanne had invited him to dinner, an invitation he'd declined rather clumsily, he feared.

But this card touched him in a way he hadn't expected. He propped it against the sugar bowl and smiled at it a moment longer. He missed her. He really missed her. He'd thought time would ease her from his mind. He'd thought Suzanne and his job would make him forget. But nothing had worked. He still felt empty, his house felt empty, and visiting her at the Mitchells, seeing her with those children, only made matters worse.

With a conscious effort he continued with the mail. Ah, well. He shrugged, pushing the stack aside. Miriam's cards usually came late, anyway—when she sent them at all.

His dinner paged him. He got up with a resigned sigh.

He'd spent the past few weeks trying not to think about Miriam and the settlement she'd received from her husband's death, and he'd especially tried not to think about where that settlement had left Kim. But fifteen thousand dollars in insurance money, a house that sold for ninety thousand and a pension of thirty thousand more proved to be a bit too much for his conscience.

Mark reminded himself that the transaction had been perfectly legal. In addition, Kim was not a minor and could reasonably be expected to fend her herself. At her age, Miriam had been in similar straits and had survived quite well. But still...!

Mark tossed his hasty meal onto the table and slumped into his chair. While Miriam might not owe Kim anything legally, good Lord, didn't she feel any moral obligation?

In contrast, Kim had never once approached him for legal advice, and he'd been readily accessible. She probably hadn't wanted him even to think about compromising his loyalties.

Mark prodded the dubious concoction of food with his fork, then took a taste. It burned his tongue. Damn! He missed Kim's cooking.

Involuntarily his thoughts returned to Saturday night at the Golden Bee and the valiant front she'd put up to look happy. It wasn't right, all that potential being snuffed out. She probably felt secure now, working for the Mitchells, and because she did, she refused to consider college. He understood. Pursuing an education would mean giving up that security. Even if she received grants and aid, the road ahead would still be hard; she'd still have to work. And it wasn't fair, especially when it wasn't necessary.

Maybe if he called Miriam. Would she listen to reason? Would an emotional appeal touch her?

Mark ate his meal, grumbling. Who was he kidding? Miriam had sent Kim packing two thousand miles just to avoid sharing her windfall. It wasn't likely she'd change her mind now, just because he asked.

Mark glanced at the phone by the refrigerator. He hadn't contacted Miriam since learning she was in Florida. He didn't know what he'd say. Or perhaps he did know and was afraid to say it. She was, after all, his sister, and the thought of losing her forever made his stomach knot.

Even as Mark stared at the phone, it rang, startling him out of his reverie.

"Hello?"

"Mark? Bob. There a seat nearby? I think you oughtta be sitting."

Out of ingrained stubbornness, Mark remained standing. "What's up?"

"I've spent the past three weeks searching for that woman you wanted me to locate. The kid's mother. Remember?"

"Yes. Did you find her?" Mark's pulse began to thrum.

"Uh, yeah."

"Where, for heaven's sake?"

Bob chuckled mirthlessly. "Queens."

"Queens?"

"Mmm. Do you believe it? She was only a few miles from her own kid and in all those years never once took an hour to go see her."

Mark squeezed the receiver, wanting to crush something. "Do you think there's any point in my getting in touch with her now?"

"Not much, my friend."

Mark's chest tightened. "She wants no part of Kim?"

"It's not that exactly. She died, Mark. Two years ago."

"Oh." Mark leaned forward, resting his forehead on the wall and closing his eyes. He would have to tell Kim, and while there might not be any emotional ties between her and her mother, he suspected she'd still feel bad.

"Well, thanks, anyway. I'm sure finding her wasn't easy."

"You'll know it when you see my bill." Bob chuckled, but his levity faded quickly. "Mark, I have something else I gotta tell you. When I started tracking Lisa—that was the kid's mother's name—I considered the possibility that she might've gone back to using her maiden name, but I didn't know what it was. There was also a chance that she'd remarried. So I looked up some records. I started with her marriage license, and from there I found her birth certificate. Well, to make a long story short, I found records, all right, but there was one I never did locate. I looked. I looked plenty. But, well, it just doesn't exist."

Mark's mouth was so dry he swallowed the dregs in his coffee cup before speaking. "And what record is that, Bob?"

The silence seemed interminable. "The one that says Lisa and the kid's father were divorced."

Mark closed his eyes and pinched the bridge of his nose. No. This had to be a nightmare. Any minute now he'd wake up.

"They never bothered to get a divorce, Mark. Which means when he married your sister—"

"I know what it means." Mark pulled out a chair and fell into it. With Miriam not really married to Cliff, and with Cliff's wife dead, most, if not all, of Cliff's estate should have legally passed on to Kim.

"It's a messy situation, Mark, and I want you to know it doesn't have to go any further than this phone call. I mean, it's bound to be a nightmare of litigation, and . . . and she is your sister. I've done my part, and if you want to forget the whole thing, that's fine by me. But if you don't . . ."

"What are you trying to say, Bob?"

The line hummed with tension. "The ball's in your court, my friend."

That's what Mark had been afraid of.

CHAPTER ELEVEN

KIM WAS SITTING on the bench along one side of the children's sandbox, reading the course catalog she'd picked up at the university, when the backyard gate opened. "Suzanne!" She tucked the catalog under her. "Are you here to see Chrissie? She's at the hairdresser's now, but—"

"No. Actually, I've come by to see you."

Me? Kim thought, bristling with wariness.

Suzanne crossed the yard, daintily kicking aside a toy in her path.

"Please, have a seat." Kim indicated a lawn chair near the sandbox. "What can I do for you?"

Suzanne sat with flawless grace, giving Kim's bare toes, wiggling in the gritty sand, a derisive once-over. "Has Mark called you this week?"

Kim had feared Mark would be the topic of conversation. Nearly a week had passed since their birthday celebration, and during that time her life seemed to have come unglued. Though she still tended the Mitchell children with her usual efficiency and loving attention, the job held no real joy for her, no sense of purpose beyond financial survival. Thinking that Mark's suggestion might be the solution to her malaise, she'd decided to enroll in a few summer courses at the university. But even this she approached without enthusiasm. With Mark from her life, her world had lost definition and faded to shades of gray. Kim didn't know how much longer she could go on, wanting him so much and feeling so horribly empty.

"Mark? Call me?" She leaned forward to help Jason turn over a plastic sand mold. "Uh, no."

"Damn!"

Kim glanced up sharply. "Why? What's the matter?"

"You haven't heard about the partnership then?"

Kim's heart skipped a beat. "No. Was it finally decided?"

"Oh, yes. It was decided."

"You don't seem too pleased. Is something wrong?"

"I guess you could say that. Mark was passed over."

"Wh-hat?" Kim couldn't believe her ears.

"He didn't get it. Stu Zambroski was promoted instead."

"Zambroski!" Kim stumbled out of the sandbox and paced in a blind circle. "How could they do that to Mark? He's the most forceful, most brilliant person in the firm—everybody says so—and they'll never find anyone more hardworking."

"I agree." Suzanne's face was mottled in anger. But Kim soon realized she wasn't angry at the three men who'd made the decision; Suzanne was angry at *her*.

"Are you finally satisfied?" Each word fell clipped and cold from the woman's lips.

"You think I'm glad he didn't make partner?"

"You certainly didn't do anything to help him. From the moment you arrived, Mark's life started to go haywire."

"I suppose you're referring to the argument he had with Milton Barnes the night of his party?"

Suzanne pinned her with a steady accusing stare.

"But Milton was harassing me. If Mark didn't succeed in acquiring Milton as a client that night, it wasn't because he was inept. It was because he chose to be a gentleman and come to my defense, instead." Even as she spoke, Kim knew that if she hadn't been at the party, Mark wouldn't have had any reason to confront Barnes. Suzanne was right. Mark's failure that night *had* been her fault.

"The incident with Milton Barnes is merely the tip of the iceberg. Or are you purposely glossing over your arrest and the notoriety Mark suffered as a result?"

Humiliation flowed through Kim, hot and thick. "My arrest shouldn't've had any bearing on the partners' decision. It has nothing to do with how well Mark performs on the job—and everything to do with the sort of man he is. I was frightened and embarrassed, and he was there for me. The possibility that he might be turning an unfavorable light on himself was the last thing on his mind."

Suzanne's eyes seemed to spit fire. "That's exactly the problem. When you're involved, what's good for Mark is always the last thing on his mind. How do you do it?" She laughed caustically. "How do you get an intelligent conscientious man like Mark to do a dumb thing like walk off the job in the middle of the day, hmm? Do you whisper self-destructive messages in his ear when he's asleep, or...or are you just extra good in bed?"

Kim's mouth dropped open in numbing shock.

"I suppose you thought we wouldn't find out about that, huh?"

"A-about what?" Kim's voice croaked.

"The fact that you went away with Mark that weekend."

"Went away? You mean skiing?"

Suzanne snickered in contempt.

"Suzanne, all this time did you think Mark left the office that Friday because we'd planned a hot weekend and he couldn't wait to get started? Good Lord, does everybody think that?" Suzanne didn't answer. "You've got it all wrong. It wasn't planned, and it certainly wasn't hot. Nothing happened." Kim gulped, knowing she wasn't entirely telling the truth. "But even if something did happen, this is the 1990s. Who cares what a person does off the job?"

Suzanne thrust herself out of the lawn chair, glowering. "My father does, that's who, especially when he believes that person is two-timing his daughter. Added to Mark's other indiscretions, that ski weekend made him question just how trustworthy a partner Mark would make."

Little Bethany began to whine. Kim scooped her up, ignoring the sand that came with her, and settled her on her hip. The awful truth was just beginning to sink in. Mark had lost the promotion, the position he'd been striving for all his adult life, and she was the cause.

"H-how's he doing?" Kim's voice wavered with worry.

"Frankly I don't know, but I'd guess terrible. He quit."

"He what?"

"Quit! Cleaned out his files and left the firm. What else could he do after being humiliated before his colleagues in such a blatant manner?" Suzanne hurled each word like an accusation.

"But... it isn't fair! Mark deserved that partnership."

"Don't talk to me about fair. Do you have any idea what this has done to our future? Someday Mark and I were going to take over the firm."

Kim's eyes widened. "As husband and wife?"

"Most likely."

"Was Mark aware of this?"

"I'm sure he was two steps ahead of me all the way. He's a very ambitious man. At least he used to be. But since you landed on his doorstep, he's become completely unfocused. I've watched him lose interest in the firm, lose interest in his colleagues and career goals, in everything that used to make him tick."

Kim's breath seemed impossible to catch. Good Lord, was she that destructive an influence in Mark's life?

"I don't know what he's going to do now," Suzanne went on, her voice catching. "He probably doesn't, either. I just went by his house, but his cleaning woman said he'd gone away. She didn't know where. That's why I came by here. I thought maybe you knew."

Kim shrugged, feeling helpless. "He's probably just gone off somewhere quiet to do some thinking." She turned away, not wanting Suzanne to see the moisture gathering in her eyes. "I . . . I'm sure he'll be all right."

"Yes, well . . . when he does return, I'll do my best to get him back into the firm and help him put his life together again. In the meantime, do him a favor, Kim. Leave him alone. I asked you to do that weeks ago, but you obviously didn't listen. Now you see the consequences. So I'm telling you again. Butt out of his life, okay?"

But I have, Kim thought, staring up at a gray sky through her tears. *I've moved out of his house. I haven't visited, haven't called, and it's been four long weeks now!*

But apparently that wasn't enough. Her heart sank. "I'll do whatever I can for Mark."

"Good. I'm glad we understand each other."

A moment later, Kim heard the gate click shut.

ONCE HER MIND was made up, Kim realized she could move mountains. Within three days, she was back in New York, and Colorado was just a memory.

Leaving had been harder than she'd anticipated. She'd come to love the area. But she refused to be a detriment to Mark any longer. Although he didn't love her, he apparently felt a lingering familial responsibility. Why else had he been so concerned with solving her job dilemma the night of their birthday party? And if she went ahead with her plans for college, he'd undoubtedly feel obliged to help with those, too. But he didn't need any more burdens or drains on his time. He didn't need *her.* And so she'd decided to leave and let him get on with his life.

The Mitchells had been quite understanding, considering the short notice she gave. They'd even written a glowing letter of recommendation for her to take to her next employer—which only made leaving more difficult. They'd grown to be her friends.

Kim had called Charlotte and arranged to stay with her until she got her own place. She'd made her flight arrangements, packed her belongings and, before she could think twice, had been on her way. Speed had been of the utmost importance. She'd wanted to be gone before Mark returned from wherever he was. If she'd run into him, her resolve to leave would surely have crumbled.

And now here she was, yawning at Charlotte's breakfast table, just as she'd done so many times before. But Kim was far from being the same person. Even Charlotte had sensed the difference when she'd met her at the airport the previous night.

"Wow! Will you get a look at *you!*" she'd exclaimed, admiring Kim's hair.

But Kim knew the change ran deeper than her appearance. Oddly enough, having finally accepted the fact that she was alone and on her own, Kim had come to know a certain serenity. She'd developed more confidence, too, and for that she had Mark to thank. His ready belief in her had made it possible for her to believe in herself.

"Are you gonna be all right while I'm at work?" Charlotte asked now. Her parents had already left for their respective jobs.

"Of course. Go. I have tons to do today."

Charlotte scraped back her chair. "You sure you don't want to come into Wheeler with me? Your replacement's a real airhead."

Kim smiled. "Thanks. Not today. I have a few other leads to follow first."

"Okay. See you at five then. And, hey, it's good to have you home."

"Good to be home," Kim returned.

Charlotte paused at the door. "I know you don't mean that now, but you will. Give yourself time."

Kim hoped she was right. Old friends, familiar surroundings—she hoped that was all she needed to heal her ailing soul.

Kim spent the day running errands. By the time the bus dropped her off that afternoon, she'd registered for two summer courses at City College and applied for eight jobs. She'd forgotten how tiring East Coast humidity could be, forgotten, too, the noise and dirt, the crush of people. As the bus rumbled off, spewing its thick exhaust, she rubbed her hands over her eyes. Her skin felt gritty.

Heading up the sidewalk, she tried to smile. She should be proud of all she'd accomplished this day. Instead, she only wondered why she still felt empty.

Maybe Charlotte was right and she just needed to give herself time. For all she knew, this hollowness might simply be jet lag.

Nevertheless, Kim purposely took the long route to Charlotte's house, the route that went by the old duplex where she'd grown up. She didn't know why she wanted to see the place now, but she did. Was it a desire to return to her roots? she wondered, as the peeling gray structure came into view. Did she think it would somehow ground her? Give her a firmer sense of being home?

She came to a stop in front of the convenience store across the street and gazed at the house that should have been hers. Strange curtains hung at the windows. A tricycle was tipped on its side on the front walk. Kim longed for a moment of high emotion—ranting resentment or tearful melancholy— anything to fill the void inside her. But nothing came.

Two teenage girls in black biker jackets walked past her just then, giving her a slow interested appraisal. At first Kim smiled on the chance that she knew them, but the look in their eyes soon convinced her to start walking again. In the opposite direction.

She was dressed all wrong for a stroll down this particular memory lane. In her going-to-interview suit, she must look like a lost tourist. Kim walked on, not caring that the girls were now a full block away. She still felt unsafe.

But right before she rounded the corner, she paused to take one last look at the house. She didn't belong here anymore, and realizing the fact, she turned away with relief.

Her feet were dragging by the time she reached Charlotte's street. And then her steps came to a dead stop. Someone who looked impossibly familiar was sitting on the front stoop. Kim curled the fingers of one hand through a chain-link fence to steady herself. It couldn't be him. It couldn't.

The man was sitting forward with his head in his hands, as if the weight of the world was bearing down on him. But as Kim resumed her unsteady pace, he looked up, straightened, and she knew she'd never think anything was impossible again.

CHAPTER TWELVE

"MARK?" Kim's incredulous voice quivered. Slowly he got to his feet. In her emotional muddle, Kim's composure crumbled. Her eyes welled up, a sob convulsed her throat, but just as abruptly she found herself laughing.

Mark walked toward her with a loose stride and a slow smile. Kim pulled in a deep breath and willed herself to calm down.

He stopped a foot in front of her, thumbs hooked into his back pockets, and with a wry look around drawled, "So this is Brooklyn."

Logically Kim knew his being here made no sense at all, but emotionally it felt absolutely perfect. "I know this is a dumb question, but what are you doing here, Johnson?"

"Would you believe I was just in the neighborhood? It's the truth. Almost."

Kim couldn't take her eyes off him, he looked so good. She wanted to touch him to make sure he was real.

"What are *you* doing here?" he inquired.

"I live here. Remember?"

"Not the last time I checked." The humor left his eyes.

"Yes, well—" she fidgeted "—I decided to move back."

"Hmm. Paul told me. I called there today, hoping to speak to you. You could've knocked me over with a feather when I learned you were here—that *we* were here, in the same city. Is there any particular reason for this move?"

Kim shrugged evasively. "It's home."

Mark's eyes darkened with an emotion she couldn't peg. "But... without even saying goodbye?"

"I planned to call. Listen, would you care to take this inside. My feet are killing me and—"

"Not really. We have a lot to discuss and I prefer not to be disturbed." He glanced at his watch. "Come with me, Kim."

Her pulse hammered. "Where?"

"Out for a drink. Dinner. I'm staying at a hotel in Manhattan. We can go there." He noticed her hesitation. "Please, Kim. It's important."

She didn't like the sound of this. "Shall I call us a taxi?"

"Not necessary. I'm driving a rental."

For the first time Kim noticed the sedan parked at the curb. She sighed in resignation. "Okay. Let's go."

They kept the conversation light on the drive out of Brooklyn—street directions, complaints about traffic—but as they approached midtown, the tension between them heightened noticeably. Kim couldn't imagine what Mark wanted to talk about, unless it was to lambaste her for having finally done in his life. Her breathing, despite her efforts to be calm, grew increasingly shallow and rapid.

Once they reached the Park Avenue hotel where Mark was staying, he left the car with an attendant and escorted Kim inside, across an elegantly appointed lobby toward a bank of elevators.

"Hold it." The idea of being alone with Mark in a hotel room shot a bolt of panic through her. "You said a drink, maybe dinner...."

"Kimberly, I want to talk, nothing more." The doors opened, and with a firm hand on her back he urged her forward.

Kim's cheeks warmed. Of course he only wanted to talk. How presumptuous of her to think otherwise. How embarrassing to reveal what was on *her* mind.

Mark's room was large and luxurious, decorated in art-deco tones of ecru and black. Two long windows looked out toward Central Park.

"What would you like to drink?" he asked, unlocking the liquor cabinet.

"Club soda's fine." She had to keep her thinking clear.

Mark crossed the pale plush carpeting to hand her a glass, then with slow deliberate moves placed his own drink, Scotch, on a table and sat. "I don't know where to begin." A thoughtful frown etched his brow.

Pacing, Kim studied his reluctance. "If this has anything to do with Stu Zambroski getting the partnership, don't hedge. I've already heard. I also know you quit the firm as a result." There. She'd said it. Just jumped right in and broken the ice. Now Mark could get on with his tirade.

Instead, he only looked confused. "The partnership? That was the last thing on my mind. But since you've brought it up... Come sit. You're making me nervous."

Kim sat, dazedly placing her glass on the table that separated them. "The *last* thing? Mark, aren't you angry?"

"Why the devil would I be angry?"

Kim didn't know where to settle her gaze. "Well, because I upset your life and got you into trouble. I monopolized your time, and—" she ducked her head "—I made you lose the position."

"Oh. So it was all your fault, was it?" He grinned. He actually grinned.

"Mark, how can you sit there so calmly? It was your job. Your career!"

"No, kitten. It was only a dream that came up empty. You know about such things, I believe." He flashed her a heart-stopping smile. "When I was young, financial security seemed the most important thing in the world to me, an attitude I can justify only by saying I grew up in abject *insecurity*." He hesitated a moment before adding, "As did Miriam.

"So I went into law, and when I passed the bar, I set my sights on only the fattest, most prestigious firms in town. Oh, I told myself I'd chosen law for idealistic reasons—justice, social order, that sort of thing—but the motives that drove me back then weren't entirely noble. I saw partnership in one of those firms as the ultimate assurance of financial security and social success.''

Mark leaned toward her, forearms on the table. ''But it didn't take long before dissatisfaction set in.''

''Dissatisfaction? You?''

''That's right. More and more I realized I was a pretty capable person, a real asset to the firm. *They* were lucky to have *me*. I also became aware that I'm a person who dislikes doing other people's bidding. I like to set my own pace, be in control, pick my goals—and my battles—and usually none of those issues has a damn thing to do with a client's net worth or my social or financial security. Somewhere along the way, Kim, values and ideals kicked in.''

Kim smiled. ''I have a feeling they were there all along.''

He shrugged. ''Maybe. All I'm sure of is that recently some of the things I was expected to do became a battle of conscience.''

''Like pandering to Milton Barnes?''

''Mmm. That's not what I want my life to be, Kim.''

Kim warmed with pride in Mark, a pride that never seemed to stop growing. ''Then, you wanted to leave?''

He nodded stolidly. ''I have another flash for you. I didn't quit because they promoted Stu Zambroski. I'd already handed in my resignation, before they made their decision.''

The muscles of Kim's stomach fluttered. If that was so, Suzanne had fed her misinformation. Deliberately?

''Do you think they would've offered you the partnership if you'd stayed?''

''Yes. I know it for a fact. They told me as much when I resigned, hoping to keep me on. Do you think they want me as a competitor?''

''Is that what you intend to become?''

''I plan to start my own practice, if that's what you mean.''

Kim was sure she was grinning from ear to ear.

Mark smiled, too, but only halfheartedly. "Looks like we're both starting new ventures, doesn't it?" He avoided her eyes and gazed out the window, instead. "So, are you going to be pushing a baby buggy out there one of these days, or what?"

Kim didn't know what to make of Mark's deliberately flat tone and lack of expression. "Actually, no. I did some thinking about what you said. You know, about college? And I've decided to give it a shot."

Mark turned. "That's wonderful, Kim."

"Of course, getting a degree's going to take awhile, because I'll be working full-time but, heck, what else am I going to do with myself? So it takes me seven or eight years. What would I have at the end of that time if I didn't go to school?"

She got to her feet and walked to the window. She couldn't bear to sit there anymore, looking at Mark and talking about the future. Without him, her future stretched ahead of her, barren and bleak.

"You still haven't told me what you're doing here. Suzanne told me you'd left Colorado Springs. Is this where you've been? She didn't know."

"She wouldn't. Suzanne and I . . . We aren't seeing much of one another these days."

Kim's head swung around, her heart lifting with hope.

"And to answer your question, yes, this is where I've been. Here and Florida."

"Florida?"

"Yes." Mark swirled the amber liquid in his glass. "I saw Miriam."

On legs that threatened to give out, Kim returned to her chair. "H-how is she?"

"Right now? Not too happy."

"Is something the matter with her?"

Mark looked at her squarely. "Kim, you may get a little peeved with what I have to say, but please hear me out. For the last month I've had my friend, the private investigator, checking on a few details about . . . about your past.''

Kim's eyes snapped wide open.

"What he found out is that . . .'' Mark looked genuinely anguished now.

"Spit it out, Johnson.'' Kim hoped her flippancy disguised how shaky she was.

"Kim, your father and mother were never officially divorced.''

Her stomach bottomed out. "Are you sure?''

"Yes. Absolutely.''

"Then, what about him and Miriam?''

"A bigamous marriage.''

Kim reached across the table and in one swallow emptied Mark's glass of Scotch.

That was only the beginning of the roller-coaster ride, she soon discovered. Mark went on to tell her much more. Too much more. She could barely take it all in. Apparently, her mother had lived in the neighboring borough all the time she was growing up, a fact that hurt more than learning the woman had died two years ago. But the most startling news of all was that, with Miriam not legally married to Cliff, she, Kim, was entitled to his entire estate.

"That's why I flew out here. I wanted to check the exact wording of the various documents that named Miriam as your father's beneficiary.''

"But . . . her name was on the deed. I saw it.''

Mark shook his head. "A bigamous marriage automatically severs tenancy by the entirety and creates tenancy in common.''

Kim suspected she looked more baffled than ever.

"Trust me. Upon your father's death, at least half the house should've become yours. If we can also prove that Miriam exerted undue influence on your father and entered the marriage through fraudulent inducement, then the other half's yours, too, kitten, along with everything else.''

Kim clutched her head. "I'm very, very confused.''

Mark smiled sympathetically. "It won't be easy to unravel this mess, but I *will* do it."

Kim was beginning to feel light-headed. "You say you saw Miriam?"

She watched his expression sadden. "Yes. Once I was sure of my facts, I flew down to Florida and confronted her with them."

Kim rose out of her chair again and went to stand at the sun-warmed window, staring dazedly over the pale May greens of the park. She was quiet a long thought-filled moment, dreading to ask the next question. Mark came to stand with her.

"Mark, do you think she knew? Was Miriam aware that my father wasn't divorced when she married him?" Mark touched her shoulder, and she couldn't help leaning into his warmth and strength.

"Oh, she knew. That's why she was so eager to send you packing. She was afraid if you stayed in New York you'd find out. She got especially nervous when you went to that free-advocacy group."

Kim reared back. "I didn't tell her about that."

"She found out, anyway. You left their number by the phone."

Kim groaned. "And that very week she came up with the idea of moving to Colorado."

"That's right. But it was only a ruse to keep you from stumbling upon the truth."

"Gee, and I thought she sent me out there because she just wanted to keep every cent for herself."

"She did. But her greed was compounded by the fact that it was outside the law."

Kim shuddered at the depth of Miriam's malice toward her.

"The irony is, if she'd been just a tiny bit generous, if she'd sent you to me with the money for school as she'd promised, and maybe a few months' rent, she might've gotten away with her scam. A couple of thousand buck's

would've hardly put a dent in her bankroll, yet you would've been set up and I wouldn't have felt so responsible.
My getting involved in your life led directly to investigating
Miriam. Her greed blinded her, Kim, and in the end was her
undoing.''

Her undoing. The words scraped along Kim's conscience
like a jagged fingernail. ''What's going to happen to her
now?''

Mark sat on the windowsill and, taking her hand, urged
her forward to stand between his legs. It was a gesture of
intimacy that made her weak. Still, his movements were restrained, his expression neutral, and whether he was acting
as uncle, friend or lover, she couldn't tell.

''That depends on you, Kim. I've done the groundwork.
All I need is your okay to proceed.''

Kim felt she was standing on a pinnacle in a very high
wind. ''And everything Miriam inherited will be taken away
from her and given to me?''

''Yes. You'll finally be able to do whatever you want. You
can go to school without having to worry about money. You
can devote yourself full-time to your classes, enjoy a social
life, maybe even travel a little on breaks, just the way a stu-
dent should.''

Kim shivered through a laugh as all the possibilities
opened out before her. ''And Miriam's not going to put up
a fight? *That* I can't believe.''

''She won't. I took the liberty of implying you'd press
criminal charges if she did.''

Kim withdrew her hand from his, comforting as it was.
She lowered her head, feeling the winds of her emotions
buffeting her on every side.

Finally she looked up and gazed steadily into Mark's
waiting blue eyes. ''Forget it, Mark. I don't want the money.
I can get along just fine on my own.''

Mark shot up off the windowsill and gripped her arms.
''Are you crazy? That money's rightfully yours. It's your
legacy.''

"If so, it's a pretty sad one. A real legacy isn't money or...or things. It's the love, the values a person's left with. It's the memories and sense of family. At least that's the only sort of legacy I've ever been interested in."

Mark released her and thrust his hand through his hair. "Dammit, Kim. I went through a lot of trouble on your behalf."

"Yes, you did." A smile quivered on her lips. "And I value your effort far more than any settlement that might've come as a result. What I still don't understand is why you did it. Whatever caused you to go against your own sister?"

Mark didn't hesitate. He cradled her face in his hands and looked deep into her eyes. "You were more important, Kim. I couldn't bear the idea of someone hurting you the way she was. She'd already robbed you of seven years of your life. She wasn't going to rob you of any more."

"But...Miriam deserves a break, too. Her life wasn't easy."

"Don't you believe it. She ran off when things got tough on the farm, and then, instead of going to school or work, she made a career out of marriages. Each one left her a little better off than she'd been before entering it. Right now she has an eight-room pink stucco house on an acre of canal-front property, a pink Coupe de Ville to match, and a sixty-two-year-old husband in the latter stages of emphysema."

Kim gazed at him blankly, conjuring up an image of Miriam in her new life. She half smiled, in pity. "I see. Well, maybe she and I can settle out of court. A compromise or a sharing of some sort. And you needn't be involved." Turning the tables on his sister had to have been the most difficult decision of Mark's life, and Kim didn't want to make his situation any more painful.

Mark's thumbs sensuously stroked the curve of her lips. "But I *am* involved, and I *will* stand by you through whatever happens."

Tears pricked at the back of Kim's eyes. Her throat worked convulsively.

"Because as far as I'm concerned," he said, "family is where you find it, and from here on in, it looks like it's just you and me, kid."

The tears that had only been stinging now spilled down Kim's hot cheeks. On an impulse, she reached up and wrapped her arms around his neck. "Oh, Mark, thank you."

Contact with his body, brief as it was, had a cataclysmic effect on her senses. She backed off quickly and stepped away. "S-so, is that all your news? I truly hope there's nothing else." She attempted an indifferent smile.

Mark's eyes narrowed, measuring her reaction. He nodded. "That's all." The finality of his tone made her heart sink. "I'm happy for you, Kim. You'll finally get the break you deserved long ago. You'll be on your way." He turned to the window again and stood looking out, grim-faced.

Kim hooked her hands on her hips and stared at him with deepening curiosity. He looked almost as dejected as she felt. Not having a clue where her boldness came from, she suddenly said, "I'd like to move back with you, if you don't mind. I much prefer the university in Colorado."

Mark didn't move. From the utter stillness of his shirt, Kim suspected he wasn't even breathing.

"Then why did you move back here?"

"I . . . I thought I was bad for you. I thought you'd be better off with Suzanne. But now I see I might've been mistaken, and . . . and if housekeeping is still an acceptable exchange for room and board . . ."

She'd never seen him look so despairing as he turned his gaze on her upturned face. "Kim, don't tempt me."

"I'm not kidding. Unless you don't want me there."

"Don't want you?" He made a low strangled sound deep in his throat and the next moment pulled her into his arms. "The trouble is I want you too much, kitten." He crushed her to him as if he'd denied himself a vital need too long. "And it's not fair."

"Not fair? What are you saying?"

Mark smoothed his hands down her back. "You're young...just starting your life. It isn't right for me to tie you down. You'd get bored, restless. Soon you'd start resenting me."

Kim was beginning to like the sound of this. Breathing in his spicy warmth, she suppressed a smile. "You, Mark Johnson, have the screwiest imagination I've ever encountered."

He cocked his head, looking slightly offended.

"What makes you think I'd be happy pursuing a life without you?" she asked.

A light of something like hope sparked in his eyes. "Until now, your life's been awfully restricted. Soon you'll have the means to travel, meet people, do things you've never done before."

Again, instinct took over. She wound her arms around his neck and snuggled closer. Lord, it felt good to be with him again. "Mark, do you feel old or inadequate compared to me?" She smiled irrepressibly.

"Hell, no!"

"Well then...well then..." She reached up on tiptoe and pressed her lips to his. It was the boldest move she'd ever made, but somehow she knew her life, their life, was hanging in the balance.

Mark tried to resist, but soon his defenses crumbled. She felt a heat building between them, and then he was fitting his mouth over hers in a kiss that was pure possession. When they finally broke apart, he was breathing raggedly.

"This is a terrible situation," he said.

"The worst. And I want you to know I'd like it to continue. There's no place I want to travel without you, Mark, nothing I want to do that wouldn't seem empty if you weren't with me to share it." Kim waited, watched his eyes, caught somewhere in space and time.

Slowly a smile teased his mouth. "You're sure?"

"Quite."

His smile broadened as he folded her closer. "Then I think you'd better give your friend Charlotte a call and tell her you won't be back tonight."

Kim pulled a face of mock outrage. "Is that so?"

"Uh-huh." Mark lowered his head, slanted his mouth over hers and kissed her with a thoroughness that left her reeling.

"In the meantime—" he scooped her off her feet "—we have a few things to do here that may take a while."

"Like what?"

He kissed each of her eyelids and then her nose. "Let's see. I've never told you how much I love you. I figure I'll have to spend at least an hour doing that. And then I have to ask you to marry me, and you have to think up an appropriate answer."

Yes. *Yes!* Kim's heart sang.

Mark lowered her to the bed, the satiny coolness of the ivory spread sliding beneath her body. As he joined her, Kim's pulse thumped with an excitement and a happiness she'd never known before.

Lying by her side, Mark propped his head on one hand and simply gazed at her, not touching, not speaking. The humor that had filled their banter slowly ebbed, leaving him serious and adoring. "I love you, Kim. I have forever, but for one dumb reason or another, always denied it. But no more. You're the best thing that's ever happened to me, and I want to share my life with you, have children with you..." He paused, his eyes darkening as the full implications of his words hit home. "Children. Oh, Kim, can you imagine?"

Kim laughed on a sob as all of life's possibilities blossomed silently, invisibly, between them.

"Please say you'll be my wife. These past few weeks without you have been pure misery. I know we had a shaky start, but it took less than twenty-four hours for me to re-

alize you were one special lady, and I'd be honored...
Please, will you marry me, Kim?''

Kim's eyes welled up, and for once she didn't even try to
stem the flow. ''Yes,'' she cried. ''Of course.''

THROUGH THE OPEN BEDROOM window, Kim heard drifts
of backyard sounds—people talking, occasional laughter,
a string quartet playing Bach. Her breath fluttered like the
wings of a hummingbird.

''There, that oughtta do it,'' Chrissie mumbled around a
mouthful of hairpins. Standing on a footstool, she gave
Kim's headpiece a gentle tug.

''Am I done?''

The tiny blonde stepped off the stool. ''Oh, Kim!'' Her
voice caught on a sob of unexpected emotion. ''You look
like an angel.''

Kim turned to the mirror and sighed a soft ''Oh, my!''
She couldn't believe that the beautiful glowing bride reflected there was really herself.

Because she and Mark had wanted to be married as soon
as possible, they'd decided on a small home wedding. But
somehow, with Chrissie's assistance, ''small'' had turned
into ''elegant.'' Instead of the tea-length dress Kim had
planned to buy, she now wore a floor-length confection of
beaded satin, tulle and alençon lace, the sort dreams are
made of.

Chrissie, a shimmer of mauve chiffon and beads, handed
Kim her bouquet. ''Okay, love, it's time.''

Mark had expressed doubts about having the ceremony in
the yard, but with the help of a professional landscaping
crew, Kim had transformed it into a garden fantasy, the fo-
cal point of which was a white arbor entwined with pink
roses. From the sun porch, she gazed toward that arbor
now, past her seventy-five seated guests, past the potted tree
roses, hanging baskets and musicians. The minister was
waiting there, along with Paul Mitchell...and Mark.

Kim's heart thumped wildly against the heavy beading of her gown. Dressed in a gray cutaway coat, Mark looked, well, magnificent! She bit her lip, wondering how a street kid named Kim Wade had gotten so lucky.

The musicians caught Chrissie's signal and began the wedding processional. Kim lifted her chin and stepped out into the late-afternoon June sunshine, her eyes fixed on Mark. He hadn't looked toward her yet, and for one brief moment she wondered if he was having second thoughts.

And then he turned, and even from a distance she saw his composure shudder. Why, he almost looked on the verge of tears. But the expression melded so quickly with a smile that Kim figured she'd imagined it.

The love burning in his eyes flooded her with warmth. When she reached the arbor, he took her hand and together they faced the minister. Her heart felt near to bursting.

The ceremony proceeded smoothly. Vows were spoken. Rings were exchanged. And finally the minister was saying, "You may kiss the bride." Mark did, resoundingly, much to the delight of their guests. Kim emerged from his embrace blushing.

Immediately friends gathered round to offer their congratulations. Waiters spilled from the house, bearing trays of champagne and hors d'oeuvres almost too beautiful to eat.

"A lovely ceremony. Quite touching," several women commented. And, "How did you pull together such a splendid affair in so short a time?" Admiration and acceptance shone in their expressions.

Everyone from Brightman, Collins and Fuller was there, including the senior partners, who Kim was pleased to see held no rancor toward Mark for leaving the firm. Their good wishes for the couple's future seemed genuine. She glowed with pride. Mark was truly an amazing person to have made so controversial a move and yet command such respect.

Suzanne was there, too. Not inviting her had seemed small-minded. And during a rare moment when Kim was standing alone, she approached. Kim tensed.

But Suzanne surprised her. "I hate to admit it, but Mark looks really happy." For a moment she looked peeved, but then a smile flicked through her grudging expression. "Congratulations, Kim. I wish you all the best. You're obviously just what he needs. I . . . I was wrong." She ducked her head and hurried away, leaving Kim gaping after her in surprise.

"When are these people going to leave," Mark complained in Kim's ear, long after the reception had moved indoors.

Kim kissed his turned-down mouth. "We obviously throw one heck of a party."

"Yeah? Well, I've got a honeymoon waiting to get underway." His eyes crinkled, burning with affection. "I love you, Mrs. Johnson."

Mrs. Johnson. Kim's eyes welled up yet again.

Apparently Chrissie caught the exchange. "Time for the bride to throw her bouquet," she announced. "Then we can all call it a night."

After their guests departed, Kim and Mark climbed the stairs to their room, quietly talking and laughing about their day. But it wasn't over yet. The next morning they'd be flying down to Mexico for a week's vacation, and they still had some packing left to do.

"There. I think everything's finally done." Kim zipped her suitcase closed with a satisfied smile.

"Not everything." Mark caught her elbow and spun her to him. "Isn't there a rule somewhere about how long a person can wear a wedding dress?"

Kim spread her hands on Mark's pleated shirt and pressed into his warmth. As he fumbled with the pins that secured her veil, she answered, "I do believe you're right, Mr. Johnson." A moment later, the veil sighed to the floor.

Sometime during the night, however, Kim awoke, feeling a vague unease that something had *still* been left undone. She slipped out of Mark's warm embrace and tiptoed to the window seat on the far side of their room. There, bathed in moonlight, she opened her journal and poised her pen. But the day had been so full, she didn't know where to start. Her mind drifted and, instead of writing, she simply sat, listening to the peace that filled her home.

Across the room, Mark lay slumbering. His hair was tousled, his jaw slack. His strong muscled back rose and fell in a steady rhythm, his arm still reaching where she had lain.

Kim swallowed, a sense of life's wonder and magic suddenly overtaking her. Less than three months ago, she'd been as alone as a person could get, and now her happiness filled her completely. Mark was the most admirable man she'd ever known, and the life they would build together would be rock-solid, peaceful, and yet as exciting as a trip through those vast twinkling stars overhead.

Kim gazed down at her journal, the page still blank except for the date. Never had she felt so deeply the inadequacy of words to express what was in her heart.

When she finally closed the book, she'd managed to write just one brief line. With a shrug and a sigh, she unfolded herself from the nook and returned to bed.

The book lay on the window seat, opalescent with moonlight. Within its pages, ink was drying on the simple words: There are some perfect days.

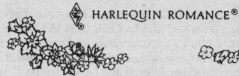

WIN-A-FORTUNE
OFFICIAL RULES • MILLION DOLLAR SWEEPSTAKES
NO PURCHASE OR OBLIGATION NECESSARY TO ENTER

To enter, follow the directions published. **ALTERNATE MEANS OF ENTRY:** Hand-print your name and address on a 3″×5″ card and mail to either: Harlequin Win-A-Fortune, 3010 Walden Ave., P.O. Box 1867, Buffalo, NY 14269-1867, or Harlequin Win A Fortune, P.O. Box 609, Fort Erie, Ontario L2A 5X3, and we will assign your Sweepstakes numbers (Limit: one entry per envelope). For eligibility, entries must be received no later than March 31, 1994 and be sent via 1st-class mail. No liability is assumed for printing errors or lost, late or mis-directed entries.

To determine winners, the sweepstakes numbers on submitted entries will be compared against a list of randomly preselected prizewinning numbers. In the event all prizes are not claimed via the return of prizewinning numbers, random drawings will be held from among all other entries received to award unclaimed prizes.

Prizewinners will be determined no later than May 30, 1994. Selection of winning numbers and random drawings are under the supervision of D.L. Blair, Inc., an independent judging organization whose decisions are final. One prize to a family or organization. No substitution will be made for any prize, except as offered. Taxes and duties on all prizes are the sole responsibility of winners. Winners will be notified by mail. Chances of winning are determined by the number of entries distributed and received.

Sweepstakes open to persons 18 years of age or older, except employees and immediate family members of Torstar Corporation, D.L. Blair, Inc., their affiliates, subsidiaries and all other agencies, entities and persons connected with the use, marketing or conduct of this Sweepstakes. All applicable laws and regulations apply. Sweepstakes offer void wherever prohibited by law. Any litigation within the province of Quebec respecting the conduct and awarding of a prize in this Sweepstakes must be submitted to the Régies des Loteries et Courses du Quebec. In order to win a prize, residents of Canada will be required to correctly answer a time-limited arithmetical skill-testing question. Values of all prizes are in U.S. currency.

Winners of major prizes will be obligated to sign and return an affidavit of eligibility and release of liability within 30 days of notification. In the event of non-compliance within this time period, prize may be awarded to an alternate winner. Any prize or prize notification returned as undeliverable will result in the awarding of the prize to an alternate winner. By acceptance of their prize, winners consent to use of their names, photographs or other likenesses for purposes of advertising, trade and promotion on behalf of Torstar Corporation without further compensation, unless prohibited by law.

This Sweepstakes is presented by Torstar Corporation, its subsidiaries and affiliates in conjunction with book, merchandise and/or product offerings. Prizes are as follows: Grand Prize—$1,000,000 (payable at $33,333.33 a year for 30 years). First through Sixth Prizes may be presented in different creative executions, each with the following approximate values: First Prize—$35,000; Second Prize—$10,000; 2 Third Prizes—$5,000 each; 5 Fourth Prizes—$1,000 each; 10 Fifth Prizes—$250 each; 1,000 Sixth Prizes—$100 each. Prizewinners will have the opportunity of selecting any prize offered for that level. A travel-prize option if offered and selected by winner, must be completed within 12 months of selection and is subject to hotel and flight accommodations availability. Torstar Corporation may present this sweepstakes utilizing names other than Million Dollar Sweepstakes. For a current list of all prize options offered within prize levels and all names the Sweepstakes may utilize, send a self-addressed stamped envelope (WA residents need not affix return postage) to: Million Dollar Sweepstakes Prize Options/Names, P.O. Box 7410, Blair, NE 68009.

For a list of prizewinners (available after July 31, 1994) send a separate, stamped self-addressed envelope to: Million Dollar Sweepstakes Winners, P.O. Box 4728, Blair NE 68009.

SWP-H493

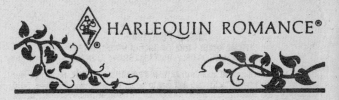

HARLEQUIN ROMANCE®

welcomes you

BACK TO THE RANCH

Let your favorite Romance authors take you West!

Authors like Susan Fox, Debbie Macomber, Roz Denny,
Rebecca Winters and more!

Let them introduce you to wonderful women and strong, sexy
men—the men of the West. Ranchers and horsemen and
cowboys and lawmen...

Beginning in June 1993

Wherever Harlequin books are sold.